To the Island

Meaghan Delahunt

GRANTA

Granta Publications, 12 Addison Avenue, London W11 4QR

First published in Great Britain by Granta Books, 2011

A CIP catalogue record for this book
is available from the British Library.

1 3 5 7 9 10 8 6 4 2

ISBN 978 1 84708 063 9

Typeset by M Rules

Printed in the UK by CPI William Clowes Beccles NR34 7TL

For Francis

The Crossing

1

The traffic was loud in the rush of a Piraeus morning. Her small son trailed behind her, fresh from sleep and still rubbing his eyes. With her free hand she dragged their case across the cracked footpaths. They headed away from the station towards the harbour, past the African vendors with their bags and watches, past the stray dogs and one-eyed cats and the men selling *koulourákia* from small carts. She was exhausted now and couldn't get warm. Lena silently practised her Greek and hid behind her sunglasses, her scarf wound tight as a bandage. She found her son's hat in his pocket and insisted he wear it. She could see he wasn't happy. Over there – she pointed to a kafé at the edge of the water, trying to cheer him – not far now.

Inside herself a hard wind tugged at abandoned buildings, a black sea cut the horizon; all the people gone.

Where are we going? Alex was tired after the long flight and the three days in Athens and the strange hotel. He was tired of the crowded streets and the early starts. Tired of looking for someone he'd never met.

You know where, Lena said, trying to ignore the pull in his voice. I told you yesterday. To catch a ferry.

But why?

To see your grandfather.

Johnny? He was needling her.

Not Johnny, she said. You know that.

I don't want another grandpa.

Johnny's gone now. Lena stopped and turned round, forcing people to fold about them. He's not coming back.

Alex glared at his mother, torn between tears and argument. He stood there with his arms crossed, people arrowing past. Then he rubbed at his eyes again: Can I have my game?

She was relieved. Sure, kiddo. As soon as we sit down.

Lena felt bad, fobbing him off with the computer game, but she had no energy for further explanation. If she couldn't fully justify this trip to herself, she couldn't justify it to him. *Why are we here?* She slumped into a seat just inside the door of the kafé, ordered a coffee and a hot chocolate. Yesterday, their third day in Athens, they had begun their search for Andreas. *The other grandpa. Her birth father.* It'd been a long cold day. She'd been to Athens twenty years ago and her memory of the place was very different. Plaka, the old area under the Acropolis, was cleaner than she remembered, more beautiful, but more tense. They'd arrived out of season, she told herself, in difficult times. Just down from the designer shops, thin Bangladeshi men huddled at Omonia Square trying to keep warm. There was a police cordon around a whole city block of asylum seekers. Near Monastiraki station, junkies traded favours. That was it, Lena realized. As if Athens had been renovated, painted bright colours, but the edges left raw. They'd avoided barricades near Syntagma and then collided with a demonstration. People with placards bearing the face of a young boy. She tried to make out his name, *Alex Grigoropoulos*. In late December he'd been shot by police, she'd read about it back home. The protests had been ongoing. They'd dodged police with perspex shields and young men in balaclavas. The ground was full of broken bottles and tear-gas canisters. *Jesus. What are we doing here?* Lena had asked herself. They'd pressed into a doorway waiting for it to pass, as if sheltering from a storm.

Yesterday they'd learnt that Andreas wasn't in Athens but he was alive still, this birth father, they'd learnt that much. She opened her bag to check that she had the piece of paper. She worried about losing it. They could try this address, the relatives had said. They could go to the island.

In summer this harbour kafé would be full and the waiters would scythe around tables. For now they were the only foreigners and the waiters were in no hurry. There was a Greek priest and his family at the next table and an old man with a walking stick opposite. The old man took sips from his small cup and clicked *komboloi* beads in a regular soothing rhythm. Alex looked up from his game. The old man held the string of beads up to the light, smiled and beckoned him over. Alex stood up, took a few steps forward and looked back at Lena. She could see that he wanted to go. He was drawn to fathers and grandfathers; drawn to men who could show him the world of men. He missed Johnny terribly, Lena knew. It's OK, she said. Go on. *This is Greece*, she thought, taking the measure of the man, *that ease with children.*

The old man gave Alex a demonstration and then gave him the beads. In his small hands they resembled a rosary. She looked over and smiled as her son twirled the amber beads and the old man lit one cigarette after another, watching him with delight. Everyone was framed in great haloes of smoke and she longed to join in. She hadn't smoked for two months.

Still early days, Lena reminded herself. What more could she expect?

The ferry loomed into view and Lena went over to get Alex. The old man smiled and pressed the *kombolói* into her son's hands. In Greek and then English he said: *Éna doráki yia séna.* For you, a gift.

Lena could see that the beads were old and well used. Something precious.

Thank you, but no. Really, we can't ... She tried out her best Greek.

Take it, he said.

Really?

Vévea. Of course.

You're very kind, she said. What do you say, Alex?

Efharistó, said Alex. Thank you. The one Greek word he knew.

Bravo! said the man. His Greek is very good. You are from?

Australia, said Alex.

So far away, said the man.

So far away, Alex echoed and looked out across the water as if home might suddenly appear. As if Australia could be brought closer by looking.

Lena thanked the man again, in Greek, but the old man waved the thanks away. *Típota!* It's nothing! *Kaló taksídi.*

Alex waved. What'd he say, Mama? he leant in, whispering.

Good travels, said Lena.

Kaló taksídi! Alex called back, a perfect mimic, holding up the beads. He had a way about him that could shatter her heart. She resisted the urge to clasp him and never let him go.

They waved goodbye to the man again and pushed up the ramp along with everyone else. The harbour kafés had emptied and there was a crush onto the ferry. There were plumes of exhaust and the racket of trucks and cars and scooters. They were trampled by the priest with his wife and children, elbowed by old women with boxes of sweets. Alex ripped his sleeve on a bird cage and lost his hat. He kept tight hold of the *kombolói*. When they got out on deck the horn sounded, reverberating right through her. She loved that sound – the long deep blast of it. Once upon a time, she would've felt that sound at her centre. She would've known how to move to it. Now she wasn't so sure. She wasn't sure of anything.

Out on deck, the wind strafed her face and hair as she buttoned Alex's jacket and then her own. She hugged him to her. A thin haze of pollution hung over the port. She remembered this yellow haze – the *néfos* – being much worse twenty years ago. They stood next to an old woman leaning out, waving to her grandchildren as Piraeus grew small. Lena presumed they were grandchildren. The woman wore black and Lena thought she must be a widow. But perhaps the woman was mourning someone else – a brother or a sister or an aunt. It wasn't just widows who wore black here. In Greece the bereaved were not hidden away. She envied them their visibility and acknowledged place. For some months now she'd felt she should be wearing black. She wondered whether time really did heal or whether these women still found themselves in the quiet hours in a place of burnt trees and tired earth, where no grass grew, only stones. She wondered if, like them, she would ever seam-over, scar-up and maybe one day find herself in a warm place, a different place, in the right season.

*

On the ferry she'd booked non-smoking seats. The smokers had their own section but smoke filtered through and the old cravings were back. She settled Alex and herself in the Economy seats and looked around. At this time of year the boat was half empty. There were a handful of older mountain people, plus the priest and his family. Itinerant workers and truck drivers and a blind man selling lottery tickets. There was the family with the bird cage and a well-dressed couple with a small boy. Lena and Alex were the only foreigners on the boat.

She looked towards the smoking section at the older men lighting up, and wondered if her Greek father smoked. She wondered – not for the first time – what he really looked like. She hoped he'd recognize her instantly and claim her as his own. It was the Disney version, she knew that, and for years it had cocooned her like a blanket.

He had disappeared. That's all she really knew.

As a child she imagined what this could mean: a man rising into the sky on a sea of balloons; a magician sawing someone in half – a piece of silk across an empty box – gone!

Other times she imagined a man walking off the end of the world. Walking and walking. Away from the shoreline of her mother and herself. As she grew older, looking at grown-ups – the shape of them, so solid and sure – how could a man be there one day and not the next?

At times when she could see that her mother might be caught out, might yield something different, she'd ask, What happened to him? Where did he go? Always the same questions. In a supermarket aisle, say, or after dinner, just as she was tucked into bed, she'd slip the question like a knife into skin. It was something she'd learnt early. To get in quick because the knife went both ways.

He disappeared. He left us. Always the same response.

Didn't he love us? Lena was insistent. Didn't he want us?

Her mother would say, Shhh now. That's enough. Time for bed.

For years – all the years of her childhood – the disappearance seemed to her as strange, as miraculous even, as water into wine at Mass. To understand it was like finding shapes in clouds or trying to make sense of dreams.

*

Once out of the harbour, about an hour into the trip, the day turned. The sea became rough and the sky dark as if it had absorbed all her feelings and cast them back. She hadn't thought this whole thing through. *We may not find him.* Here she was, with this address in her pocket, and they were on their way to an unfamiliar place. She couldn't fool herself that this was a holiday. She wondered if her Greek were up to it. If she were really up to it. If her stepfather Johnny were still alive she wouldn't be here on this ferry going to this island, that was for sure. It was as if the accumulation of years, of who she was and where she lived and what her life was about had gone with him. Inside, she felt as if she were falling. One thing after another. A year of blood and loss, that's how she saw it. Certain years brought you to your knees. Left you winded, alone on the stage, never wanting to get up. A *stage?* She frowned to herself. She hadn't been near a stage in a long time, didn't know why that image should come now to disturb her.

It was six months since her stepfather's death, two months since her own operation. She still felt in a continuous present. She still expected Johnny to come round a corner with a certain look on his face, say something to make her laugh, scoop Alex up to show him some marvel of nature or machinery. Lena was eighteen months old when her mother married him. Her earliest memory was of walking towards the front door, unsteady, holding her mother's hand. His large shadow behind the frosted glass. Johnny knew he'd been Catherine's second choice and he'd made peace with it. She'd loved someone else – some foreign bloke, she told him all about it – and been left high and dry. He didn't care. It was as if he'd won first prize in a chook raffle. He felt lucky to have stumbled across her – ten years his junior. Plump and blonde and pretty. So clever, so independent. So different from his ex-wife, for he was still smarting from the mistake of his first marriage. In his eyes, Catherine could do no wrong. He loved her and she gave him a hard time for it, but he thought he'd been given another crack at life. That's the way he put it.

Why is she so mean to you? Lena once asked. She must've been six or seven then.

Johnny stopped what he was doing – always something with cars – a whole stack of bits and pieces in the front yard. He wiped his hands on his trousers and bent down to lift her high in the air. It's just the way she is. But it's still love, *Tangles* – he always called her *Tangles* – it's still love. And he'd look back towards the house, to the room with the closed curtains where her mother lay in one of her moods, as if it were a sacred site.

He was always tinkering – mooching – according to Catherine. He'd take apart shonky things and fix them. He had an eye for the mechanical. He had an eye for the broken-down, the irreparable. He could make anything work again. He ran his own garage and then on the weekends, as a hobby, he did mates' cars, fridges, televisions, you name it.

He could've won the Nobel, her mother would say, half-joking. But he never got an education.

I finished school, Johnny would counter. His voice easy and low, not wanting to cross her. He was always quietly spoken.

University of Life, huh? At that point, inexplicably, her mother would come over and kiss him on the forehead. The best university there is, she'd say.

You betcha.

And they'd stand there a while, like two large ships nudging up against each other. Her arm around his shoulders, him leaning in with the illusion of safe harbour. Then her mother would pull away and draw out the words like a gun. Shooting him when he least expected it – *No substitute for the real thing* – she'd pull away suddenly and retreat to the lounge. Sharp words split in her wake. There was no humour or irony in her voice: *I'm the brains of this operation.*

You're the brains! Johnny would call back.

At these times, Lena would see the cloud pass his face, so at odds with the cheer in his voice. The way he would grip the newspaper. Take a deep breath. There was the gap between how someone seemed and what they actually said. She became alert to this gap. She learnt that you could fall into it, do yourself harm.

After the day's work Johnny would sit at the kitchen table barefoot in his singlet and Stubbies and pour himself a beer, with his newspapers and books about him – he was a big reader – happy as a lark. That's how her mother would describe it, as if larks were a terrible thing. As if the condition of larkness, simple happiness, was something foreign.

This is what it's all about, Cath. He'd push back from the table, arms out, enveloping the room, the kids, the mess, the suburb, Melbourne, the universe.

Put a shirt on, Catherine would say.

My wet blanket. No malice in the voice, he'd go back to the *Evening Herald*.

You're pissed.

I'm happy. I'm just showing you how happy. And he'd jump up from the table and swing her around, kiss her on the neck, the whole time she'd be pushing him away.

Not now, Johnny!

Lena could see that in their own way, they were content.

Years later, when Lena had learned some Greek, she would frame it like this: Johnny had *kéfi* – a great enthusiasm for life. As for her mother – who knew what'd happened? She'd lost it. Simple as that. Johnny was spontaneous and easy-going. Her mother was volatile and uptight. Somehow they made a couple, made a jagged whole. Like a picture puzzle, the shapes cut to make some kind of a family.

She couldn't imagine being coupled-up, in for the long haul. Her own relationships never lasted and she thought it was a mystery, what made a couple tick.

Johnny said that all people were a mystery, what made them tick.

A two-bit philosopher, her mother would say.

The days when Catherine was not speaking made Lena want to leap and spin or somersault to get attention. She would leap from chair to chair, trying to get around a room without touching the ground. She would jump off the sofa, off the back veranda, wanting to fly. Sometimes she'd stand at the window with her hands on her hips, still as a statue, copying her mother.

Cut it out, Lena, Catherine would snap.

Lena would turn around with her hands on her hips. A perfect mirror image. She'd made her mother speak! Lena would put her hand on her heart and extend it to Catherine and offer her an invisible flower. She learnt early that words could break or hurt or wound. You had to be careful with them. Sometimes you needed another way to say the same thing.

Such a show pony! Catherine would exclaim, half-admiring, half-reproachful. Where did we get you from? My little entertainer, her mother would say, almost affectionately. What will become of you?

*

Lena looked out at the dark water rushing up. They were out into the deep now and the sky lowered itself to the boat. She tried to reconstruct Johnny from snapshots in her mind. From holidays and birthdays and good times. In the evening, before she went to sleep she tried to imagine him at the beach, at a barbecue; happy frames to cancel out the final one.

Lightning and thunder. An electrical storm and the sea was a great animal shaking off its pelt. It reminded her of the storms of her childhood. The static in the air, the way she could feel it in her hands and feet; how her hair would frizz up. The way it made her want to move. As a child she always wanted to run into the thunder, to raise up her hands; to do cartwheels. She felt the old urge but the thunder felt different. She couldn't work out what the sound wanted from her and she had no energy. Since the operation, sounds vibrated differently inside. She felt all hollowed out. She was going to have to learn all over again. How to move, how to listen.

Since Johnny's death it was as if a wall had come down in the family house – the wall that held the whole thing together.

The water churned and rose and fell; great black sheets washed over the windows. Alex became seasick along with everyone else. People coursed along the shiny floors and gripped the metal handrails trying to get to the bathrooms. People slid around like toddlers – thrown back on another way of moving. She smiled to herself. *Every move a dance step.* She held Alex by the waist; everyone around them was green-faced and miserable. As soon as the waves took hold and the old ferry started to roll, as soon as she was on her feet and trying to flow with it, she felt her mood lighten. It was the movement, she realized. She smiled again and it dawned on her that she was enjoying herself, for the first time in a long time, trying to keep balance, sliding the waves. *A sea ballet.* Shapes and gestures formed themselves. She could see the steps in her mind and she wanted to follow. With an effort she brought herself back to her son, clasped him tighter and stroked his head, trying to soothe him.

Alex was unhappy but it was more than seasickness. He hadn't wanted to leave Australia. To leave his friends at kinder. He hadn't wanted to leave his grandmother. Lena tried to sell it to him as a big adventure. But she knew that it was her adventure, really. That she was taking her child along for the ride.

Pretend you're a cowboy, she said. Walk like this. And she showed him how to keep his balance – to walk like a dancer, feet splayed.

He smiled wanly up at her. But Mama, he said, I'm sick.

Be a sick cowboy, then, she tried to soften, but her tone was frayed and he knew it. You couldn't hide anything from a kid.

She'd booked their tickets and rented out the house in Melbourne. She'd got another three months off work. Sick leave. She could extend it if she wanted. She'd packed lightly with everything in one case. She was a good packer – a legacy of her touring days. They would maybe make contact with this birth father or maybe not. In the great Australian tradition she'd come overseas looking for the past. She was here to find her roots.

Or end up rooted, her brother said.

She'd laughed at that. They'd both laughed. The old words from their childhood. *Rooted. Stuffed. Cactus.* All the ways to say that something was spent. Then another image came, another meaning. Suburban boys in panel vans, one arm on the wheel, slowing down at the sight of a girl, *Wanna root?* She wondered if Alex would turn into such a boy. What kind of man he would become. The way her mind ran. *Rooted.* Who the hell used that word any more?

She was on some sort of a mission, all this movement, after the year they'd had. Surely it must be a good thing?

In the middle of this storm at sea, music came over the tannoy – snatches of bouzouki – and Lena felt the sound spread across her shoulders. Alex was now heavy and sleepy against her and she leant into him and briefly closed her eyes.

The night before they left Melbourne, she'd had a dream of two fathers. That's the way she read it. Her stepfather Johnny had walked through this dream raising a glass of beer in a toast, *Yeía mas*, he said inexplicably in Greek and sat down and smiled at her. He pointed through the window. She could see a man just outside with his head bent, a spade in his hand, digging. A small white church in silhouette and the sea beyond that. She started weeping, although why she couldn't say. It was only in dreams she allowed herself to cry. The man kept digging and refused to look up. She called out, but he refused to answer. When she woke, the dream was still fresh, unwilling to release its hold, and the pillow was damp.

*

In Australia, Lena had a Greek first name and resembled someone she'd never met. Here, looking around the ferry, Lena resembled just about everyone. People with dark hair and Byzantine eyes. Faces that hid nothing. Despite this, she didn't feel at home, or at ease. Not at all. The whole thing was a whim, a distraction. Her mother had been right about that. They'd argued the night before she left.

Ridiculous, her mother had said. This whole idea. Catherine moved around the kitchen, shifting pots and pans, scrubbing the dark spot behind the sink that she always scrubbed in bad times. She'd cared for this daughter and grandson for two months since

Lena's operation. For sure, they'd kept her going in the long slow days after Johnny's funeral, when everything is done and the person is gone and there's no turning back. But they were both hard yakka, this daughter and the grandson, she'd be the first to admit. Now that they were leaving, the kitchen felt huge and she had visions of herself adrift and alone with a dish towel in hand, scrubbing at her own reflection.

Let sleeping dogs sleep, she said, her voice raised. You don't need to go anywhere now. You need to rest.

Keep it down, said Lena.

She listened out for Alex. Worried they might wake him. Alert to his murmurs and night fears. She left the table, her mother still angry, and went up to stand in the doorway of her son's room. Reassured by his regular breathing she took one last look – checked the night light – he'd needed it these last months – and partly closed the door. He needed light and open doors now in order to sleep. These days, she rarely slept. She struggled with herself; she must try to get some rest. Coming back down the stairs, she said, What's so wrong with going to Greece?

Nothing's wrong with Greece, her mother said, turning away. Everything's wrong with him.

Lena soothed: I may not find him.

You will. Her mother was adamant and resigned at the same time. If he's there, you will.

The address in Athens was on an old postcard. It's in Exarcheia, she said. Not far from the centre. Not far from Plaka. Maybe someone will know where he is. She couldn't bring herself to say his name. My friend Marsoula sent it. Lena had looked in the Athens phone book online but there was no one listed under his name.

Lena knew what it cost her mother to give her that address.

I may not find him, Lena said again, trying to be kind.

You can't rely on him, Lena.

I won't.

Believe me. Even if you do find him – he's not a person to rely on.

But Lena was stubborn, never listened, Catherine said. Besides, Lena wanted to put this year behind her.

First the blood, each month worse than the last. She'd put off the operation as long as possible. There were many reasons. Johnny was ill. Catherine needed help. Lena was used to pushing through pain and difficulty. It was her nature. Her dancer's body was used to it. Then there were the strange associations from her youth: the Catholic women with their children lining up for Communion. Mrs Costello or Mrs Riley. She remembered some of the names. Long lines of children and the mothers at the end of the line. Months when the women would disappear and the kids would front up with some other family member. A father, say, or an auntie. If you went to visit, to play with these kids, you were told to keep quiet because the mother needed rest. A while later the mother would reappear at Mass and Lena could remember the adult whisperings in the porch. No more kids for Maria, they'd say. No more kids for Alison.

In pre-pill days a hysterectomy was Catholic birth control.

No more kids for Lena. The thought cut her open. Lena wasn't even sure if she wanted another child. But she wanted that possibility. She didn't want it taken away from her. She'd stalled the operation as long as she could.

If you go on the pill, I'll know.

When Lena was a teenager, her mother had been full of such warnings. A pregnancy was the worst that could happen. That was the message. But you could do nothing to prevent it. Even though Lena found her mother's pills one time in the linen press. Her own mother had been on the pill! But Catherine became increasingly conservative as she grew older. She observed all the feast days, not just Easter and Christmas. She became a parish woman orbiting the priest, arranging the flowers, making herself useful. She became increasingly devout as Johnny pulled amicably in the opposite direction.

It's not worth it, Lena, for three minutes of pleasure.

Who's counting?

Please. Don't make my mistakes.

I'm not a mistake.

That's not what I meant.

When Lena did get pregnant, it was, inevitably, a mistake.

She was thirty-six years old at the time. She'd been fond of Gil and they'd worked together at the local primary. She'd taught dance and he taught PE. He'd been a friend. And then one Friday they got together after a work's night out. Too much drink and too little food and the next thing she knew, weeks later, the line on the test changed colour and a one-night stand meant something else. Gil had a girlfriend and it was hard, but they tried for a while after Alex was born, to be a family. It just didn't pan out, her and Gil. She still felt bad about it. They were better as friends than as lovers, that was a fact. That's how she thought of it.

You're too strong-willed, her mother said at the time. You can't leave a man with a baby in tow.

Watch me, said Lena.

Gil married his girlfriend, moved to Sydney and had two children. He stayed in touch at birthdays and Christmas and sent the occasional cheque.

It was the fate of all couples to separate. Lena accepted this. That's what life had shown her. *I will leave you one day. Whether by accident or design. One day we will come apart.* A person could walk, could choose someone else. Could disappear, even, like her birth father. That was one way. Or you could stay with someone forever and then lose them. Her mother was a widow now after the long years with Johnny. She felt alone, at a loss, Lena knew this. There is no template for happiness, she thought. Who reads about a happy couple? There's a template for getting together and falling apart. The old story. But the opposite? Life held no clemency for happiness or good behaviour; for good long years together. The fate of all couples was to be separated. To be beached somewhere eventually, pale as driftwood.

When she saw couples now – happy, sad, warring, wrapped up in each other – she felt no envy. She could only think of how it would end.

She'd been a single mother all this time and Alex was almost six. The way his birthday fell, he could've started school early but she'd decided against it. Now they had this time together and she was glad he'd start next year. After he was born, she'd gone back to teach at the primary, kept going to dance classes and workshops when she could. Kept the choreography going in her mind. Her dream had always been to have her own studio. Her own dancers. She'd seen a perfect place in Fitzroy shortly before Johnny died. It was a run-down place along a blue-cobbled lane. In summer the datura flowers hung heavy and sweet over the fences, creamily narcotic. It wasn't far from the Housing Commission and the Aboriginal edges of the city. When she'd told Johnny about it he said that they could do it up themselves. He would fix the roof and restore the floorboards. Install the mirrors and open up the windows, let in the light. He'd been full of the idea. Now was the time to do it, he'd said, even when he was breathing only with oxygen and finding it hard to climb the stairs.

For months he'd been ill. He lay there with his bad chest and inside the cells multiplying, dividing; his lungs like honeycomb. He'd smoked all his life but was fit as a fiddle, everyone said. He wasn't old. So many things could kill you. It was a wonder anyone got out of bed in the morning. He was a smoker, said the surgeon, what could you expect . . .

Life isn't fair, said Catherine.

Lena stayed quiet and dry-eyed. She didn't know whether it was fair. She didn't know what to feel.

20

You're a tough cookie, said her mother. You've always been tough.

One of us has to be, Lena thought. That's always been my job.

Lena took two Temazepam the night Johnny died. She'd found the tablets in an old rucksack. She'd been hoping to sleep right through. But she woke early with a heavy head, bleeding heavily. Everything felt cold and then she remembered – this is how it would be from now on. And this was only the first day, the day after. Johnny would never be in this day. And it hit her full force like a wave: a wave that she couldn't dive under, a wave that she couldn't avoid, and then Alex called out, and he came in crying for his grandfather.

Where's Grandpa?

He's not here.

Dead? He said this point-blank and it shocked her.

Yes.

It's true?

He's not coming back.

No? He couldn't believe it.

Never, she said softly and she drew him to her. She lay down next to him, stroked his face.

We have to get used to it, she said.

For the first few weeks after the funeral, Lena felt chill and small. She wrapped her arms around herself, and for the first time ever, had no desire to move. The bleeding got worse. By contrast, her mother found new energy. Cleaned the house from top to bottom. Couldn't stop moving or talking. Lena watched her mother carefully. *Movement never lies.* Lena learnt this as a young dancer and it came back as she watched her mother shift dust around the kitchen. She seemed capable and calm but the line of the shoulders and the mouth told the true story: her mother was all bent out of shape.

Lena was like a poker player, alert to the tells of human gesture and movement: the too-steady gaze; the pained smile; the tight jaw. *To see the truth you have to spot a lie.* Dance taught her this.

She'd always watched her mother closely. There were things about her that Lena could never soothe or fully understand. Catherine was taller than average, heavy set and fair. Her shoulders stooped as if life had dealt her more than one blow; as if she still expected to be hit at any time. She seemed at war with herself – all instincts and impulses – all played out at the dinner table. Over the years, Lena watched her mother's struggle to be thin and thought that this was what it meant to be a woman – food was out to get you – something deadly and serious. Mealtimes became a game of push-pull. Lena pushed food around her plate. Her mother urged her to eat. It was a game neither of them could ever win.

*

She watched a Greek family unpack their lunch on the ferry. Tupperware vats of food lined up like a military operation. The food spread across two tables. The grandmother produced plastic plates and napkins and cutlery. Soon the whole family sat around forking food in their mouths and passing loaves of bread as if they were in their own home. None of them appeared to be seasick. In between platefuls, the adults tapped out cigarettes, laughing and joking. Lena wasn't hungry but she longed for a cigarette. She watched the women at the table at ease with themselves and their children.

Her own mother had never been at ease. Catherine had always been prone to sudden squalls of mood. As a child Lena remembered the frenzied bursts of cleaning at 3 a.m. and days when the house smelt of bleach and disinfectant. Other times, dishes piled in the sink and the bin filled to overflowing, the house smelt of rotten peel and sour milk. Johnny trying to keep on top of it all. They lived off omelettes. Baked beans on toast. He'd cook black pudding and fried tomatoes. He made sure they ate fruit, had clean clothes. Every night he'd line up their school shoes and buff them to a shine. She could see him now: Johnny putting out clothes on the Hills Hoist, his mouth full of pegs; the only man for miles who knew how to cook, how to clean and how to care for kids. Lena remembered weeks when her mother rarely left her room. Johnny would place toast and mugs of tea outside the bedroom door. There you go, love, he'd say. Lena would hear her mother's voice telling him to leave her be. The toast and tea would remain untouched but then Lena would stumble upon Catherine at strange times of night. Just the outline of her mother in the blue light of the fridge. Standing in the kitchen, spooning butter into her mouth, drinking cartons of milk, hiving hunks off cheese. Lena would make herself into a shadow, press herself flat into the wall and turn to walk on tiptoe back to her room. Not wanting to disturb. Not wanting to make things worse.

The ferry listed to one side and Lena could see everything in slow motion: people struggling back to their seats; the sliding plates of food; the tipping birdcage; the smoke drifting through.

She looked out of the ferry window. Here, travelling to this island and feeling the pull of the waves, she realized how little she knew or understood. About family. About anything. You knew less as you grew older, she thought. Everything becomes less certain. It became harder just to put one foot in front of the other. There was a time when she could trip over and conceive of it as a dance step. Now she was too fearful to fall. She could break a bone; her right ankle was less strong than her left, her hips ached a little. She knew how long it took to heal up. Yet children moved so freely and bravely. You could spend a lifetime trying to recapture that.

Be an island, she would say to her class.

Move like water.

And now here she was. Waves against the windows, the boat trying to steady.

I'm in Greece, she kept telling herself. I'm going to find my father.

2

On the boat, Alex stirred and said he felt cold and so she put her jacket over him. She rubbed at her sore feet and at her right Achilles – the old injury which often gave her trouble. These past three days they'd walked all over Athens and the footpaths had been worse than she remembered. As if certain areas had sunk, waiting for a final seismic jolt. It was part of the edgy charm of the place. When she'd stayed in Athens twenty years before, she'd shared a flat with other dancers. They'd had a week-long residency on a European tour. She'd wandered the streets of Plaka every spare minute, practising her Greek. She'd been too busy to find her birth father; she'd had no inclination to find him then. There was a show to put on. Besides, Johnny was her father.

All these years later, she realized that the only show involved herself and her son. How long could she perform the role of the capable adult? She felt overwhelmed. She looked at Alex and tucked the jacket more tightly around him. Try to sleep, she soothed. They were both tired after the days in Athens that had led them here, to this boat, headed for this island. On their first evening in Plaka, as they'd walked down to the flea markets of Monastiraki, it had struck her that when you return to a place you carry with you all the places and people, the petty tragedies and triumphs of the years in between. She'd felt heavy with it. She'd reached out to examine a bottle of olive oil and she could see her younger self admiring a similar bottle, perhaps even at the same stall. She'd put down the oil and realized what she really wanted was to put down the burden of those years in between.

On the second day in Athens her throat had felt tight, her abdomen had ached and she'd wanted to put off the search for her father. To distract herself she'd taken Alex up to the Acropolis. She'd once read that more people had wept here than at any other famous site. She wondered how you could calculate such a thing and imagined a pool of tears by the entrance. But she understood the power of the place. On that first visit, years before, she'd wept when she came here. She'd wandered the streets looking up every so often, seeing the Parthenon at all angles and at different times of day. Its great columns never disappointed. Sometimes you couldn't see it at all for the pollution. Then you would look up and seem to stumble across it, hovering over the city, edging through the cloud. The place had endured. Since the fifth century. First as a site to Athena, then as a Christian cathedral. It had been a mosque and an ammunitions store. It had withstood occupation by the Ottomans, pillage by the British and invasion by the Nazis. The Acropolis would endure beyond one human life. Beyond your own life. Of course it would move you to tears.

On the third day in Athens, after a disturbed sleep, she couldn't put it off any longer. She'd decided to go to Exarcheia. Now or

never, she'd said to herself. The trolleys and the buses were still
on strike and so they'd walked all the way down Patission and
then turned right at the Polytechneio building – a Greek flag
fluttered blue and white above its steps, banners hung limp from
the wrought-iron fence. They made their way up towards
Exarcheia Square. Behind the Polytechneio was a large burned-
out store. Graffiti covered every square inch: *Alexi, these nights are
yours*, she translated quickly – it was a reference to the December
shooting. They walked up the hill through piles of fallen leaves
and plastic bottles. There were a few smashed windows and street
lamps. A sign for a computer shop hung off its cables. It was a
Sunday and most of the shops were closed with heavy metal
grilles over the front. Alex loved the graffiti but some of it fright-
ened him. There was a bat with red eyes that seemed to leap out
from the wall and a death figure with eyes that followed him up
the street. To Lena, the place had a 1970s feel. Exarcheia was a
famous student area and they passed young people in black – a
cross between punks and hippies. Young men with shaved hair
and pigtails and Peruvian jumpers. Young women in short skirts
and boots with flowing hair. Her guidebook said the area had
become gentrified. In 1967, not long before the Colonels came
to power, her mother had come through Athens. She'd answered
an advertisement on a kafé wall in Plaka for English lessons. She
started teaching a girl called Marsoula in Exarcheia and, through
her, met Andreas. And this is how a single life flows, Lena
thought, her calves aching as she climbed the steps. A life flowed
from chance meetings. The whole thing a flip of a coin years ago

which led her to be here now, at this moment, in Athens with her son.

Grandma lived here once, she said to Alex.

Where?

I don't know, exactly. Somewhere near. Lena gestured around, unsure. Catherine always avoided the topic.

They approached the main square. A few junkies hung around doorways, syringes at their feet. Exarcheia Square itself was a dry grass plot ringed by benches. Under the date palms at the far end of the square two African men stood with DVDs stacked on a blanket. Men sat on the backs of the benches, drinking beer. Waiting. A scagged-out woman sat on a red parka selling tissues. There was the sound of car alarms and two-stroke engines. The place had the feel of night although it was only late morning. The air vibrated, everyone waiting for something to happen. Lena skirted the square and chose a kafé that was all pale wood and large windows. It reminded her of a place in Melbourne. She went in and took the old postcard with the address out of her bag. She showed it to the beautiful woman at the counter. It's close, said the woman, directing her down the street to a terra-cotta building. Down there, the woman said. Opposite the Hotel Exarcheion.

Lena thanked her and walked further on, past a row of kafés and two men slumped on a bench. One man held a rope attached to a large dog with a studded collar. The other man lay comatose with headphones hanging from his neck. The dog growled at Alex and she felt his small hand tense. They walked on a little more until they came to the building. She looked up. Its neo-classical facade would once have been grand. Pigeons now roosted under the eaves on the third floor. All the second-floor shutters were closed. Black graffiti ranged across street level. Lena looked at the name next to the main buzzer.

Is this it? Alex tugged at her hand.

Maybe, Lena said. I'm not sure. Lena smoothed down his hair and hugged him. She'd realized suddenly that she had to be careful what she said. She didn't want to give too much away. *If he's not there, don't say we're looking for your grandfather.* She bent close to his ear. *It's our secret.* She pressed the buzzer.

But why?

Just because. She hesitated. I'll tell you later.

But . . .

Just then a short man came to the door. For a moment, Lena couldn't breathe. No, he said. No. He was not Andreas Psarakis. Lena relaxed a little. He was a cousin, he said. But what could you want with Andreas? His tone was friendly but guarded.

We're relatives from Australia. My name is Lena and this is my son, Alex. Lena continued on in Greek. She spoke too quickly and tripped over her words. We had an old address. From my mother's friend. She paused. Marsoula?

You are from *Afstralía*? He bent down and ruffled Alex's hair.

A small, wary woman emerged from the hallway behind him.

I am Lambros, he said, then, half turning, This is Fotini, my wife. She smiled at them. This is Alex and Lena. He turned back to his wife. From *Afstralía*! They are looking for Andreas.

The woman's smile fell. Andreas?

They know Marsoula!

The man stepped back, almost colliding with his wife, who seemed reluctant to move. Come in, come in, he said.

We thought maybe he still lived here . . . Lena trailed off.

Lambros led them into a rarely used front room. The room was dark. He found a switch and a table lamp pooled gold in one corner. The furniture gleamed brown against the yellow wallpaper. He opened the curtains. There were black vases with plastic flowers on top of polished sideboards. A gilt mirror over an ornamental fireplace. The room was cold and Lambros went to get a heater.

Andreas! he muttered to himself.

Alex looked up at Lena for direction. He was confused. Why couldn't they say *father* or *grandfather*? He didn't know why she hadn't said this straight away. What to make of the big world in which big people didn't tell the full story? A world in which they told half-truths and half-lies. They couldn't tell which was which. Meanwhile, Fotini retreated to the kitchen and returned with a tray of small coffee cups and plates, a jar of *gliká* and small spoons. For Alex she brought in a special tray of Coca-Cola and biscuits. When they were all settled, after they'd discussed the Metro and what they thought of Athens, what job Lena did, how old Alex was and where did they live in *Afstralía*, how much did she earn and where was the husband, once all of these things were out of the way, Lambros turned serious.

We haven't seen Andreas for over thirty years.

That's a long time, Lena said, trying not to show her disappointment.

Andreas was political. He looked at Lena closely. You know this?

She shook her head. He disappeared, that's all I know.

He disappeared, Fotini sniffed. This is true.

My mother was a friend of Marsoula's. She taught her English, Lena said. In 1967.

Fotini looked at her husband and rolled her eyes.

We were here until 1974. Then the trouble at Polytechneio. After that, we left. You know this story? The Polytechneio?

Lena had nodded uncertainly. More or less. She'd read about it in the *Rough Guide*.

The students occupied the Polytechneio, said Lambros. For three days. The Junta sent in tanks and many students were killed. Still, every 17 November on the anniversary, this area is closed. Lambros paused. Some Friday nights, the anarchists fight *oi bátsoi*, the cops. Especially since the boy last year – Grigoropoulos? It happened nearby, he said. The shooting.

Lena nodded. I read about it. We saw a demonstration the other day.

The demonstrations! He sighed. And it's worse now. It's been bad for some years. The young have no jobs. They go away to study and they don't come back. The 700-euro generation. They can earn more outside Greece. You see the graffiti round the square. The broken windows. What to do?

Lambros continued: This is the Psarakis family home. It was

vacant for many years. We are a small family and Andreas has no brothers. His parents and sister left for the island – this was before the Colonels. He stayed on. The place was empty when Andreas left. He looked over at his wife, uncertain how much he should say. He went to Paris ...

Paris? said Lena.

Lambros decided to skip the question of Andreas' exile. We returned to Athens. It's our home now. Sometimes, Marsoula comes to visit ...

The sister of Andreas, Fotini added.

His sister? Lena was trying to absorb this new information. Her father in France and now this.

You didn't know?

Not exactly, said Lena, straightening her back against the cushions, thinking, *Marsoula is my aunt?*

Which side are your relatives? Lambros glanced at Fotini to gauge her opinion. She looks like a Psarakis. He paused. She looks like Andreas.

His wife sniffed. The eyes, she said.

Alex shifted in his seat, Lena sensed he was about to speak and she quickly offered him a biscuit. She nudged him and pulled at his jumper and he turned to her. She tried to signal with her eyes that he should stay quiet. Here, try some spoon sweet. She put the fruit on his plate. Try it, she said, lifting the spoon. He obediently opened his mouth but his expression told a different story. As he was swallowing, she broke a chocolate biscuit in half and gave it to him. Here. Delicious. He took the biscuit, unsmiling, and put it in his mouth. Lambros and Fotini looked on with approval. Lena was pantomiming a perfect Greek mother. Eat, she said. Alex kept chewing.

We're distant relatives, said Lena, relieved that Alex had his mouth full. She took a punt. There were so many Greeks in Melbourne. On Andreas' mother's side, she continued. A cousin, who went to Melbourne. Many years ago. She threw out a common Greek name. Giannis?

Lambros looked at Fotini. There was a Giannis . . .

Canada, said Fotini, unsure. Giannis that went to Toronto?

There was the Melbourne Giannis . . .

Lena took a deep breath. Is Andreas still alive?

Vévea. He's not so old. Lambros leant forward and spooned some of the sweet onto his plate. How old, Fotini?

Fotini said grudgingly, Old enough.

Ignore her, said Lambros. She never liked Andreas.

Fotini put down her spoon. He made life difficult . . .

He must be seventy now, Lambros interrupted. Let me see. He held up his right hand, trying to calculate on his fingers. If I am sixty-five . . .

Fotini cut in: You are wanting to meet the family?

We're in Greece for a few months, said Lena. We thought, maybe . . .

They are on Naxos, said Fotini. You will find them on the island of Naxos.

You have an address? Lena tried not to sound too eager.

For Andreas? She narrowed her eyes. Maybe.

The address of his friend, Lambros said. The bar, remember?
An old address, Fotini shot back.

Reluctantly she got up to get the address book from the next
room. She moved slowly. Everything about her was heavy. They
could hear the loud opening and closing of drawers in the
kitchen.

Lambros put his palms together, looked at Alex and Lena, leant
forward and said in a low voice: We never shared his politics.
Today we are Nea Dimokratia. Never are we people of the Left,
but – he held up one hand – never did we support the Colonels.
Never did we support the dictator! Not at all. But because of
Andreas and his politics – *katastrofi* for the family! He was always
close to the Reds, always extreme. I lost my job and we left
Athens for Thessaloniki. I could not get the police clearance for
work, because of Andreas. He looked towards the kitchen. She
does not like to speak of it.

At that moment, Fotini came back with a small black address
book bound with Sellotape and string.

He is telling of that old Red? She put on her glasses and flicked
through the pages of the address book. When you find him, she
said sourly, tell hello from Athens. She copied down the address
and handed it to Lena.

He became a hermit, said Lambros. This, we have heard.

Alex finished the spoon sweet and the biscuit. His mouth was
rimmed with chocolate. He looked up at Lambros. What's a
hermit?

A man alone from other people, Fotini answered for her

34

husband. Someone who lives apart. Then, more harshly, What Greek does this? She shook her head. We like to make a *paréa*, to make company . . .

Lambros said, Enough, Fotini . . .

Lena looked at the address on the piece of paper. Anything she knew about Naxos came from myth: Ariadne, Theseus, the labyrinth and the Minotaur. She'd once wanted to create her own dance piece; Ariadne on Naxos, abandoned by Theseus. Ariadne rescued by Dionysus and making a life on the island. That was one version. In myth, the island was a place of lost and found, of exile and abandonment. Of dance and new beginnings. She tried to imagine what it would be like to meet her birth father there.

Thank you for everything, she said to Lambros and Fotini. Thank you for your time. She carefully folded the address and put it in her bag.

They all stood up and hugged goodbye. Fotini seemed relieved to see them go.

Outside the apartment block, the February wind was cold and the sun was bright. Alex and Lena both blinked after the low light of the front room.

Andreas is your *father*, said Alex, his voice full of accusation. But you didn't say.

I know. I know. But I wanted to, said Lena. Believe me. I just didn't know how they'd react.

It wasn't a big lie, said Alex, slowly, in that way of his, trying for compromise. Not really. We *are* rellies, he said seriously. We *are* from *Afstralía*.

She laughed at his Greek pronunciation. That's right, she said. We're from *Afstralía*. She bent down and tucked in his shirt, zipped up his jacket. Her abdomen still ached when she bent down or twisted. Certain movements pulled at the scar. Are you warm enough?

He didn't answer. She could see he was still a little upset.

OK, she said. Sometimes people don't tell the whole truth because the truth can hurt.

She could see him working this over. She could see he held himself back.

So, he said, changing the topic, are we going to the island?

Do you want to?

I dunno, he said, trying to seem indifferent, trying to pay her back. I've never been.

She smiled, patted his jacket and stood up. Well, kiddo, maybe we should check it out, she said. As if there had ever been any question in her mind. I guess we're going to the island.

3

Yesterday, they'd been in Exarcheia. Now they were on the slow ferry to Naxos. The bad weather was making the journey even longer. The ferry rolled on and Lena could hear people groaning. Alex was sick again and they made their way to the bathrooms. Just inside the door there was a machine dispensing tampons and sanitary pads. A pale woman stood at the machine, searching in her purse for change. *Thank God*, Lena thought, *that's all behind me now*. It was a relief to be done with it. But in the next instant, as she held Alex around the waist and swept his hair back from his damp forehead she felt something quite different: *She would never have another child*.

She bit her lip and forced the feelings down. Her emotions seemed to thrum on the surface these days and she felt buffeted by a cycle that had no obvious rhythm or result. She no longer recognized herself.

Two months ago, she'd haemorrhaged in a dance class; ended up in A&E and then surgery. It happened so fast that when she came round, she didn't know where she was. For a brief honeyed moment, high on morphine, she thought she was in Greece. Opiate dreams of Greece. She woke not thinking about Johnny, not missing him, but thinking about her birth father – the man who disappeared. She wondered if he were still alive. She'd fixated on this in a way that she hadn't since she was small and a plan slowly took shape. She would go to Greece to recover. Something to look forward to, something to get her through. Perhaps she could go to find this man, Andreas.

What's got into you? her mother said when Lena asked for tourist brochures and her old Greek books. She was feverish and drawn. Nothing, she said. Leave me be.

After hospital she went back to stay with her mother and Alex.

At the end of four weeks, she lay in her old single bed in her mother's house and gave up coping, for a time. Her dreams were milk-full of pregnancy and giving birth. She'd wake up exhausted and emptied out. The dreams were so unexpected, so visceral – her breasts hurt, her abdomen hurt. She didn't know what to make of them or what to make of herself. She lay there with the old poster of the monastery fraying blue above her bed. After the operation, all the old desire to go to Greece. Everything all mixed up. She couldn't tell any more who or what she was missing. A father she'd never known? Her stepfather? Her old womb-self? I'm a dancer, she'd tried to console herself. Something always hurts somewhere.

The ferry pushed on through the dark expanse of water. Grey and white. The sky and the sea. These were not the colours Lena associated with Greece.

As a kid, Lena thought of Greece as blue-and-white and hidden. She remembered the cards Catherine would get at Easter.

Always a long-faced saint with almond eyes. Strange stamps. It was the only time Greece was ever mentioned. It's from Marsoula, her mother would smile sadly, my old friend. Catherine would put the card on the mantelpiece for a week or so and pause sometimes in front of it, as if it were special, as if it were indeed an icon. Sometimes Lena would catch her mother looking at the postcard, turning it over, passing the edges between thumb and forefinger as if returning to a page in a book, as if she'd forgotten something.

Lena had seen the old Greeks in Coburg watering the concrete in their front yards. She'd seen them put a goat on a spit at Greek Easter – whole families out in the street watching it revolve, the children cracking red eggs and the older women in black. She knew that Greek kids, like the Italians, had extra school on Saturdays. She was glad that she'd never been brought up Greek, if it meant extra lessons.

Once, as a teenager, she'd been stopped along Sydney Road and asked the time by an old man outside a *kafenío*. First in Greek and then in English.

She'd looked at her watch. Quarter past four, she said.

Íse Ellinída? he'd asked, looking at her closely. You are Greek?

She'd looked around, embarrassed. I'm sorry, she said. I don't understand. Although a part of her understood very well.

But you are Greek! the old man repeated in English. He touched her hair. He pointed to her face as if she were a prize exhibit. Greek! He appealed to an audience of passers-by.

He'd looked back through the window of the *kafenío* for confirmation.

No, Lena had said too brusquely and hurried on, all out of kilter. She was a terrible liar. He could be my grandfather, she thought. My Greek grandfather. In rebuffing the old man she felt that she'd rebuffed a part of herself. When she looked in a mirror it was undeniable: she looked Greek. Her skin turned copper in the sun, she had no freckles and she was nothing like her fair-haired mother. She was small and slight; dark hair coiled wild about her face. As a young girl this had brought Lena nothing but grief. It was the era of mahogany tans and straight white hair. She looked different, she looked *ethnic* and desperately wished it weren't so. To her tormentors at school she threw back that she was half Irish. Not really a *wog* at all.

She had a Greek first name and resembled someone she'd never met. She'd carried the idea of her birth father like a sharp stone in her pocket – both a comfort and a hurt.

You have his eyes, her mother would say in that tone she used. Aegean eyes, her mother would repeat. Long before Lena knew what Aegean meant. Her mother would grip Lena's chin with both hands and look into those eyes as if looking into a deep well. As if she would one day find the body of a drowned man there.

I love you, she'd say, as Lena struggled in her grip.

After that time outside the *kafenío* Lena became more alert to all things Greek. She'd watch the old couples on the tram down Lygon Street, crossing themselves right to left as they passed the Orthodox church. She became attuned to the long vowels of the

Melbourne Greeks, how their accents differed from the Italians or the Lebanese or the Croats. For a time she read everything she could get her hands on. Looked at tourist brochures and maps. She was sixteen and it was a way to get at her mother. But it was more than that. As if something long-seeded and dormant had forced its way to the light. She was drawn to the blue-white posters in the travel shops along Elizabeth Street. Johnny encouraged her. He bought her a Greek–English dictionary and a cassette of *Teach Yourself Greek*. To her mother's dismay she studied Greek in between dance lessons. Johnny got a poster for her wall of a monastery built high up a mountain. The colours were vivid and clear. She could stare at it for hours. As if it contained some imprint from a time before; a place stored inside. In one corner of the poster there was a small white boat. She'd imagined herself on this boat many times, travelling across the Aegean, towards stony hills and small villages, past ruins and through centuries, to meet this man with the sea in his eyes.

She could never have imagined this electrical storm, this old ferry, her seasick child.

*

Lena leant back in her seat and tried to rest. She ached for a cigarette. She felt all cramped and sore and she couldn't settle. She hadn't stretched out properly since they arrived. She'd taken up yoga about a year ago, something to keep her strong. She went to a handrail at the edge of their section and stretched forward. From here, she could still keep an eye on Alex. He was sleeping

41

now, and no one would look at her; they were too seasick to care. She reached up, she turned side to side. It still hurt more on the left than on the right. She rotated her shoulders. She'd slept badly last night in the hotel bed. Kept raking over the meeting with Lambros and Fotini. *What she'd said. What she didn't say.*

She bent first one leg and then the other. At this end of the compartment it was all mirrors. Immediately she was back in childhood, back in the old town hall. She could see her small self bend and stretch. The tyranny of it – entering the world of the mirror – the world of comparison and striving and never-good-enough. She looked at herself now as if looking at someone else. She looked terrible. Skin and bone. Dark under the eyes. Her posture all wrong. She looked like a stick woman, something a child would draw. The doctor had said three months' recovery, minimum. You look like shit, her brother said on a visit before they left for Greece. Although Dan was technically her half-brother – Johnny was Dan's real father – they'd always been close, and she'd always trusted him. He was right, she'd come away too soon – she needed another month at least. She alternated heel and toe raises then walked back along the aisle.

She passed the ferry shop and paused at the window. It was brightly lit and full of colour. It seemed full of possibility: the promise of taking her away from herself. She decided to go in. Her nerve ends on fire as she looked back at her sleeping son.

Everything in the shop was shiny and new. She spent a while just looking. She reached out to touch a display and remembered how anxiety used to fade as her hand would close over a lipstick or a bracelet. Something small. Something big. Back when she was younger, when dancing was all that mattered, on days when she couldn't sit with herself or the pulse of her work – what she could achieve, what she hoped to achieve – she'd go *shopping*. That's what she called it. She hadn't shopped anything for a long time, not since she was a kid. But just before Johnny's death, the old impulse returned. She'd wandered through K–Mart and paused in front of a display of hair clips. Her hand closed over a barrette. It came back, how easy it would be. She had that same impulse now. It used to bring a performance high and then an after-show feeling. Like starving herself, there'd been a joy in getting away with it.

Lena's hand shook a little as she put down a T-shirt and kept scanning the shelves for things that Alex might like. She told herself that it was for Alex. She saw a small flashing pen with an image of the Acropolis and a key ring with a blue painted eye. She paid and then on her way out picked up another small random useless thing, a badge with a three-leaf clover – a football badge; she smiled at the woman at the counter, thought about taking something else, saw the cigarettes and pushed her luck. She pressed through the door, cigarettes in pocket – the pin on the badge digging into her palm. She walked slowly back to her seat. Her breath even. She'd hardly broken sweat. She didn't make eye contact with anyone. She looked down at her palm. It hadn't worked; it wasn't the same at all.

This time, she felt no rush. She felt pathetic and old, the skin on her hands thin and sun-lined as she closed her fist around the badge. She was still anxious and her throat was still tight. Her heart was full and her womb was empty. Her palm hurt and she pressed harder on the badge, knowing somehow that when the hurt stopped, the pain would still be there.

Back in her seat, she hugged her knees to her chest, foolish and small. Alex was still asleep. When she looked at him Lena felt that he was the only thing anchoring her in the present. She looked out to sea and pressed at her bloodied palm with a Kleenex.

She opened up the cigarettes and reached into her bag for the old Zippo lighter that she carried for luck. She struck it once, twice, surprised that it still worked. She stood up again and walked to the smoking section, keeping an eye on her son. She inhaled her first cigarette for over two months and the nicotine went straight through, hitting her right between the eyes, like a line of speed. In that moment she felt on top of everything. Hyper-aware. The rise and fall of the waves reminded her of a scene in Plaka on their first day: two women shaking out sheets from a balcony – shaking and folding. The rhythm of it.

She took another drag of the cigarette and her mood spiralled down. She sighed heavily. Her mind ran on a groove of days gone and directions not taken. Of course she'd had dreams. But everyone had dreams. From the time she was a child, Lena felt a terrible and beautiful compulsion to move. She'd started young, in the ballet classes at the local town hall. After that she'd won a place at the Australian Ballet School. She had talent, they

44

said. Everyone there had talent. But she was too dark, too small, more suited to the part of the Spanish princess or the gypsy girl or the harlot, so they said. Not a Giselle. Not a Juliet. She wasn't cut out for these leading roles or the constant struggle to stay so thin. She took a year off and travelled around Europe. Saw Pina Bausch in Germany and Balanchine in France and stepped sideways into a new dance. Other ways of moving. She took her classical training and broke from it. She'd been braver then. Now she wondered if those had been the best days of her life. Days of tug and pull and stretch. Days she never realized were the best.

Heavy with such thoughts, she walked slowly back to her seat. Her feet ached and she took off her shoes but kept her socks on, careful not to wake Alex as she bent forward. She wore Johnny's old socks. Catherine had cleared out his wardrobe before they left for Greece. She looked down at her feet, stretched her toes. Her feet were not pretty though she cared for them well. Her big toes were misshapen. Knuckled and bony. They were working feet, she told herself. A dancer's feet. *I could've been a contender.* She said this to herself quietly, in a Marlon Brando voice, as if it were a joke. But it didn't make her smile. Such thoughts brought trouble. These past months had shown her that. Such thoughts could only bring back a future that she never stepped into. She had to keep reminding herself that this was as good as it would get: with her much-loved only child, and her teaching. With her depressed mother and a hollow at her core.

A contender.

Pina Bausch would ask her dancers: *How do you run when you've lost something? How does a broken heart feel? Show me.* Those questions came back, with force.

She'd stayed in Europe for five years, worked with different companies.

She'd been full of potential, everyone said.

Then she'd gone back to Melbourne for a visit. Lena closed her eyes. The closer they got to the island, to Andreas, the more vivid the past became. As if the memory of that particular trip home and everything since could shield her from the future. If I got through that, she tried to calm herself, I can get through anything.

*

Lena remembered that her mother had been full of Dan and the grandchild and how someone in this family was finally making something of themselves. She remembered sitting there at the dinner table and wanting desperately to get away.

Lena's made something of herself, Johnny beamed from the end of the table. He raised his glass of beer in a toast. We're proud of you, love. Just look at you!

Proud as punch, her mother said in a flat voice.

Don't listen to her, Johnny said.

Lena picked up her fork but wasn't hungry. Tiredness hit her in waves. She pushed the peas around. She stabbed at the steak, avoiding the mashed potato.

Her mother leant back in her chair. She'd already finished her tea. She looked at Lena mixing the peas and cutting her steak into tiny pieces.

Eat that up, she said. None of that nonsense. Not again.

Cath. Please. Leave her be, Johnny said.

Lena bent to the plate but she was back in childhood. She forked peas to her mouth and looked up at Catherine. She put her fork down. This is how it has to be, she thought. This is how it's always been.

She'd stayed three weeks and lost half a stone. Going back to Australia messed with her head in a way that leaving never had. Who was she to make a life away? Who was she to stray so far from home? To think she could *be* anything? Her weight kept dropping until she could no longer stand without getting dizzy. She was referred to a South Yarra clinic. Lena did what she was told. She wanted to get better. She chewed slowly and swallowed hard. She slept. She didn't weigh herself or write calories on the back of her hand. And six weeks later when she was released she didn't have the energy to return to Europe. Not then.

She'd stayed in Melbourne, joined a local company. She'd told herself it was only temporary. That when she got back on her feet, she'd return to Germany.

A boy dancer got her some pills. Try these, he said. For a time, they really did the trick. She looked the part but eventually got so wasted she could hardly stand. The company director took her aside. This has to stop, he said. *You* have to stop.

Lena realized then that she would never dance with Pina Bausch or Rambert or Merce Cunningham again.

That part of her life was over.

Or maybe – and she'd burnished this thought in the long years since, rubbing it to a mind-sheen – maybe it'd been unravelling long before that trip back to Australia. Whether she was good enough and whether it would last and the pressure of performing. *Everything.*

She pulled herself to the present. The ferry. The seasick passengers. Alex was in a deep sleep but he stirred a little as she got up and moved to the smoking area for another cigarette. She stood leaning against the wall and blew a smoke ring, as if she were a teenager. It was starting to seem real: *I'm on my way to meet my father.* She could feel the grip at her throat. What would he make of her? What would she think of him? She looked around at the other smokers and forced herself to smile, to feel a kinship. When she was younger she'd been full of quick judgements. Quick to distinguish herself from other people. Girls who were fatter. Girls who had no discipline. But life knocks that out of you soon enough.

She'd resigned from the local company – jumped before she was pushed. She'd drifted for a year and then took up dance teaching. All that first term she'd cried herself to sleep.

Back at her seat, Lena put the cigarettes away and took the scrap of paper out of her bag with the island address. She stared at the handwriting in Greek script, taking it in. Across the aisle, there was a man with his small son, trying to fix a toy robot. The man looked as if he were used to the work of fixing and mending. He balanced on his haunches right down next to the boy. He took a small screwdriver out of his back pocket. The gesture was slow, controlled, and his hands were long and thin, scarred over. This man was beautiful to watch, immersed in his work. He reminded her of Johnny.

Her stepfather had been her real father. She should never forget it. She felt a flash of anger at him for dying, and then guilt at the thought that she was here, in Greece, looking for someone else. Not a replacement, she reassured herself. Whoever this man Andreas was, he could never be a replacement.

She realized she was lousy with forgiving and forgetting. People getting ill, leaving, dying. How could you forgive all that? She couldn't even forgive herself, didn't know where to start. But this was middle age, she thought. Time to begin. She looked over again at the boy with his father. The child had a head of fair curls like her own son. He could be a brother for Alex, she thought. Ambushed by yearning, she gripped the edge of the seat, opening up the cuts on her palm.

It was early evening by the time they got to Naxos. The wind stalked the boat. The waves were so high it took an hour to lower the ramp safely. They stood behind glass on the upper deck, looking out on the harbour. A few seagulls traced lines in the air, sliding backwards in the storm and swooping in the wash of the ferry. Lightning cracked the mountains behind the town and flashed over the islet in the harbour. A small church on the islet was briefly illuminated, seeming to float on the water. Light strobed the marble gateway out on the headland.

Look, Alex, look!

Is it some kind of a door?

Yes.

Without a building?

It used to be a temple. It's called the Portara, she said. She'd read this in their guidebook. Only the door remains.

Oh, he said. He was too sick and tired to be impressed by some old door.

They pushed down the steps along with everyone else: the priest and his family, the blind man selling lottery tickets and the family with the caged bird. Everyone spilled out onto the small quay.

She looked around at the whitewashed fronts. The light was fading now and there were few places open.

We're here, she said, taking her son's hand. They bent into the wind and he asked her if she knew where she was going. Yes, she said, although she had no idea and hadn't booked anything in advance. Up here, she said. They stopped at an entrance to a lane leading into the Venetian *Kástro*. She stood under a street lamp and got the guidebook out of her bag.

How does a broken heart feel? She asked the old question of herself, aching for another cigarette, trying to read the map, trying to keep it all together: *Show me.*

Athens, April 1967

He's listening to jazz on French radio, a book open on his lap. The words blur across the page. It's late and, although he's always been a night bird, tonight it's different: he's a nixtopoúli *in a cage, hitting up against the bars. Unable to settle.*

Three hours earlier his mood had been very different. He'd sat in a kafé off Ermou waiting for Irini. It was a beautiful spring evening, the tavernas and bars full. He had no idea of what was to happen. She came walking towards him, her dark hair like a cape over her shoulders. She kissed him and placed a hand on his arm, which he reached for but she quickly shrugged him off. She sat down and ordered a frappé as usual, then rummaged in her bag for a time. Sipped at her coffee, stared off into the distance. He asked her if anything was wrong. It's nothing, she said. Briefly he wondered if there was someone else. There was the boy, Stavros. Only a friend, she'd said. He wasn't sure if he believed her. He pushed the thought down. Told himself he was becoming old and jealous – now past thirty, ten years her senior – a caricature of himself. He remembered all these slow-motion details. And then in her direct and heartbreaking way, Irini told him that there was *something wrong. Badly wrong.*

She told him it was over. It was too dangerous and she wasn't in love with him any more. She wept and was unable to look at him. Instead, she kept looking around the kafé and out into the street. Her eyes had dark shadows and her mouth was tight. She was sure she was being followed, she said. Don't contact me again. She squeezed his hand. They could remain friends, she said. Comrades. *And then she was gone.*

He sits there, stunned. He thinks back to when he first met her, over a year before. Irini had handed him a leaflet; she'd been involved in all sorts of groups. She was articulate and political and beautiful. She'd joked with him and chided him for being uncommitted, a dilettante, not involved enough. A petit-bourgeois intellectual. *He tries to make sense of her leaving. The real reasons. The age difference? His affair with the Australian? Or had it truly become too dangerous to be seen with her? Who knew what she was involved in? Maybe it would've always come undone. There was something of the fanatic in Irini — something fierce, serrated, which was part of her attraction. So different from any other woman he'd come across. She didn't want a dowry or marriage, she said. She wanted to experience things fully and become a lawyer and one day live in Paris. He'd said they could go together and that he would support her. I don't need your support, she said.*

And then she was gone. *It's a refrain he'll return to, endlessly replay, in years to come.*

Eventually he falls asleep on the couch, their old conversations harrowing his dreams. The windows are open and the radio is

*on low and the hum of the streets rises up; he always sleeps with
the window open. Athens is a noisy city and it soothes him to
know that he is not alone. Tonight, especially, when his heart
is an empty chamber with a cold wind blowing through. At 4.30
a.m. he wakes to a strange silence from the streets and the radio
full of static. He sits up and rubs at his eyes and stretches his
left arm – he has slept awkwardly. Slowly he stands and moves
out to the balcony, leans out over the balustrade. The street is
too empty and too quiet. Something is wrong, he says to himself. He walks back inside and switches the radio station. All
static. He adjusts the volume up and then down again, wide
awake now. He grabs his coat and cigarettes and walks away
from the Exarcheia apartment towards Syntagma. As soon as
he turns the corner he sees that he is not the only one. There are
students, mainly. Some he recognizes. All woken by the silence
in the streets. There are some – true Athenians – who haven't
even been to bed yet. Anxiously he looks around for Irini.
There are low voices and everyone nods to each other. Their eyes
say everything:* Can it be? *After all the talk, the years of talk.
The conspiracies. The theories. The air is full of murmur. The
air is full of questions:*

Now, it is happening?

The election weeks away . . .

The Army?

The Right?

The King?

The Americans?

Talk jigsaws around him:

Maláka! To them, everyone's a Red . . .

They keep walking, in twos and threes. They are careful not to form a crowd. He keeps a little distance. He is not a joiner. He does not need to surround himself with people, to always make a paréa. Irini once said he was un-Greek in his aversion to crowds and groups, in his desire for solitude. He is full of contradictions, she said. He keeps the windows open to know that he is not alone and yet craves aloneness. Crowds appal him; he is the first to admit. He is better one-to-one than in a group. The closer they get to Syntagma there is the metal sound of armoured cars and tanks. In side streets they see soldiers and officers. Stalled cars and pedestrians. And this is how it happens. *Overnight. A city slides from democracy to dictatorship.*

He hesitates. Looks around. He calculates them and us. The number of tanks and the number of protestors. The calculations do not work in our favour, he thinks. He has no desire to be a martyr. He does not want to draw attention to himself. He turns and walks back quickly the way he has come. He's aware that Irini would call him a coward. All theory and no action. *He loops down the small streets from Syntagma, doubling back. Her imagined insults belling in his head.*

Tanks surround the royal palace, the broadcasting station and the central telephone office. Tanks surround the ministries. Politicians of all parties are arrested along with generals and ordinary people. Soldiers with guns and bayonets patrol down empty streets. Tourists in the Grande Bretagne come out onto their balconies, shake their heads and turn back inside, uneasy. What the hell is going on? *By 6 a.m., the centre of Athens is surrounded by tanks and under control of the Junta.*

Back in his flat the radio still crackles. He wants to ring Irini. He lifts the receiver and taps it several times but the line is dead. He wonders if she would answer him anyway. She wanted her freedom, she'd told him more than once. She is a modern woman, she said. She can't be tied to one man. The irony of it. He's been a kamáki, *a womanizer, all his adult life. He is still a* kamáki. *Even now there is a foreign woman. But it is Irini he loves. His mind turns this over and over. Again he wonders if she is perhaps with Stavros or with someone else. He hopes she is safe. At 6.30 in the morning he turns the radio on again and military music blasts through. He hears Kiria Elpida come out onto the upstairs landing. He hears her wailing and shouting, as if there has been a sudden death in the family. Over and over:* Diktatoría! Diktatoría! Diktatoría! *He hears her door slam shut.*

He runs upstairs. Kiria Elpida! he calls. He knocks at her door.

Ti na kánoume? *she says, opening the door a fraction. Then in English, as if to cover herself,* What can we do? *It is the end, she says and puts one hand to her mouth as if to stop herself saying more. She does not invite him in. They have never discussed politics directly. They have learnt the public habit of silence in uncertain times. He knows that her husband died shortly after the Civil War. He has learnt that much. She has let slip this detail from a life in which little has been let slip. Her husband was part of the Resistance against the Germans then against the British. He fought with ELAS. In 1944 he was there in Syntagma when the British opened fire. She does not have to spell it out: her husband was a communist and they suffered for it. He would see Kiria Elpida at the* períptero *sometimes and they always smiled as they reached out for the same newspaper. Giannis, the* períptero *owner would smile too. The day she told Andreas about her husband she put her hand on his arm and he clasped her old hand and reassured her. They had an understanding. They were people of the Left and she was safe with him. This is the limit of what could be said. Kiria Elpida is the most battle-worn person he knows. Through the door he sees a red checked tablecloth and a copy of* To Víma *propped against the lamp. A bronze bust of Lenin on a shelf.*

Leave me, she says. She has a way about her. He does what she says.

The radio all next day plays marching songs and music from long ago. At dusk there is curfew. Officers stand on tanks shooting at the sky, proclaiming a new order. At twenty past eight, after the national anthem, the government of Colonel Papadopoulos is sworn in. The communist threat . . . *Prime Minister Kollias begins.*

What communist threat? Andreas shouts at the radio. He stands up and then sits down again. He is outraged, shaking. The last of his cigarettes spill onto the floor. He sits there with his head in his hands, thinking it all through. The threat of the Centre Union winning the election, the threat of Papandreou to American interests . . . *He hears the King give his blessing and knows that the whole country sits hushed around radiograms. Andreas rubs his eyes. He still can't believe it is happening.* There is no communist threat.

After that first curfew he sleeps only a few hours. Wakes at dawn. Later, news leaks of the casualties. Bayonet wounds. Gunshot wounds. People, unlike himself, who did not turn back from Syntagma Square. By the next day Athenians slowly emerge as if from a siege. The cars inch by. The shops open. Life gathers speed until it seems that nothing has really changed. By the third day, only a few tanks remain. People go about their business. He sees the shutters on the periptero *pushed wide and the kiosk owner, Giannis, waves him over: Your newspapers are no longer! His eyes shine, he is full of excitement. Giannis holds up* To Víma. *It is now only four pages. The two other Left papers,* Avghí *and* Allaghí, *are closed down. Journalists are in hiding or under arrest. All newspapers except for* Kathimeriní *send pages to the censors. Left, Right. From now on, and for the next seven years, it will be all the same news. Giannis the* periptero *man says, No elections now, Professor!*

He is jubilant: We are saved from the Reds.

The professor stares at him: And now we must suffer jackboots instead.

This, to Giannis. One of his many mistakes.

*

Four months after the coup, late one August afternoon, there is a loud knocking at his door. He's not expecting trouble. He's preparing for tomorrow's lecture, 'The Ottoman Legacy'. Trouble comes always in the dark, he reasons with himself, always in the early hours. He opens the door. It is Kiria Elpida, telling him that from her window she has seen the police. They are outside, she says. Junta police, ESA, *she emphasizes.* Downstairs. You must go, Professor. *She looks up and down the hallway.* Go now! *He sees the black hem of her dress disappear up the stairs.*

He scans the room. He must be quick. He reaches for the suitcase under his desk. The suitcase packed with the important things: Depon, soap, toilet paper. A small bottle of raki; packets of coffee and sugar. Poems of Ritsos. His notebook. Always, he is prepared. He reaches for a sweater lying on a chair. He may need it. He picks up the suitcase, tests its weight, and opens the back window. He's about to climb through to the fire escape when the room explodes. Five men through the door and he's suddenly face-down, hands cuffed. He calls out. Maybe someone will hear? Shouting because now the time has come: his turn. People are sleeping and shops are shut. Siesta time. Maybe someone will hear? *He is on the floor, a boot at his neck, his pulse thumping. They search the apartment: open every drawer, every cupboard. Throw books and records. Tear the place apart.*

So many books! So many foreign books!

I teach history, he tries to protest. Books are my life. Before he can finish they stop his mouth with cloth. They put on the blindfold.

Only a communist has so many books! They throw volumes of Byzantine history, shattering the spines. Pages come loose.

They fall upon Shakespeare, Tolstoy, Sartre. They are in a frenzy, mispronouncing the foreign names. They take all the money in his wallet. Moscow Gold, *they say, though everyone knows he has no time for Moscow.*

Out into the street. Yellow light through the blindfold: a small tear in the seam. He looks up to see the curtain move in Kiria Elpida's window. He's taken to a city building. An ordinary office building. Full of people wanting everyday things. A licence, a signature, a favour. But it is not an ordinary building, he knows this. He is in Bouboulinas Street: ESA headquarters. He's dragged up a back entrance with many flights of stairs. They take off the blindfold. He finds himself in an office with three men. There is a big man − the commanding officer − flanked by a small man in a police uniform and another man in plain clothes. They accuse him of planting bombs, of speaking against the National Government. He tells them he knows nothing of bombs. He tells them he has always spoken against the National Government.

He has many books, the policeman says. Communist books.

Ah, the commanding officer says. An intellectual. He leans back and taps at the American insignia on his desk. He smiles to himself.

It's all a mistake. The professor shakes his head.

This is ESA, the small policeman says. There are no mistakes.

Then the boot hits his face.

Later − he is not sure how much later − he is taken to a room on the roof, a room overlooking Attica. He will remember that view always. The view that he held in his mind, the view that he didn't see: the changing colours of the Acropolis, how the marble swelled white and then red until there was no more Parthenon, until his eyes bled shut.

*

When he opens his eyes, it continues. It does not stop.

 The room on the roof has a bench, a rope, a few poles and iron rods. Three police stand over him. One of them takes a rod and the other two fix him to the bench. There is a noise like a generator coming from the next room. Even with that noise, he can hear human sounds. He thinks it is a woman. Then they start beating the soles of his feet.

 The professor tries to fold up, tries to count his breaths. This fálanga, *this feet-beating. The Junta's favourite method of interrogation. He remembers everything he has been told. He remembers that when it is over he must not remove his boots. He must keep moving his feet or gangrene will bite. He knows this from people on the Left. But until now, for him, it is mind-knowledge. He does not know it in the body, which is an entirely different thing. Now he learns about pain. The first lesson: pain is easier to bear with a regular rhythm but* fálanga *beats a strange rhythm. Quick and then slow. Hard and then less hard. The alternation is difficult. The alternation is deliberate. His feet swell and they tie him to the bench with ropes. They burn his arms with cigarettes. They take him to a holding cell. They force him to stand between beatings. They force him to stand on one leg. If he falls down they force him up again. This continues on and off for three days.*

After three days the hallucinations start. He sees faces in the wall of the cell. He sees Irini's face in the wall. She tells him to look closely. He sees a gap in the wall and knows this is his opportunity — he will escape through this gap! He starts scratching at the walls of his cell, trying to make the gap bigger. He stands there until his fingers bleed trying to tear the bricks apart.

They come in with salt water for him to drink.

You're a professor, they keep saying. A communist. You must know names.

The professor stays silent. He cannot feel his legs. He is cold. He has gone under. He thirsts all through his body. He is floating under the skin of himself and the voices come from a long way off.

On the fourth day, a guard comes in with a doctor. He's had a bad accident, the guard says. The doctor checks him over. How many days?

Three, says the guard.

The doctor nods. There is no alarm on the doctor's face. He has been here in this exact room so many times before. He knows the history of this bench. Its every stain and marking. *The bench as palimpsest.* He cannot look the prisoner in the eye. He has had a bad accident, *the doctor repeats.* He must rest. *The doctor pours iodine on the wounds, prescribes orange juice and then leaves. He will return with medicines tomorrow, he says. He will return soon.*

The doctor never returns.

When the professor wakes he is in a cot bed. They bring bread and a cup of water without salt. They bring orange juice. He is left alone. Another day passes. He starts to feel stronger. He starts to believe they have forgotten him. He starts to believe that the doctor will soon return and then the door opens and the same men come in from the first day. He is taken to another room, with a bench and a desk. Give us three names, says the commanding officer. Any three. We'll arrest any two you don't like.

There is a long moment and then the commanding officer picks up a piece of paper. Clears his throat. Listen, he says, they won't be ill-treated.

He throws the professor a pen. You will tell publicly how the communists led you astray. Sign here – he bends down to hand him the piece of paper and as he straightens up, he checks his reflection in the window opposite. He tightens his belt and adjusts himself at the crotch.

The commanding officer turns his back and rearranges the papers on his desk. Smiles. When you're ready, I'm ready, he says, looking up at the clock on the wall. Five minutes pass. Then more impatiently, he says: I'm waiting. He taps his fingers against the American eagle on the desk.

The professor stays mute. He ignores the pen and paper at his side. There is a long still moment and then the small policeman grabs him by the hair and throws him to the floor. The man in plain clothes picks up an iron bar.

The professor counts his breaths, hoping to go under, and hears one of them say:

Stop!

Do you know why you're here? the commanding officer says in a conciliatory tone.

The professor wants to speak but the words don't come. His feet have burst through his shoes. His face and clothes are blood.

The officer answers for him: You listen to the foreign radio. You like the foreign music, the foreign newspapers. You teach in the dimotikí *and have friends who plot against us. He points to the sheaf of papers on the desk – we have evidence from many sources. Any one of these things – the officer looks at him with a bored expression – any one of these would be enough. But more than this – you have the long hair. You have the communist face! The officer laughs hard. Just look at him! He glances at the wall clock and then over at the two men. Looks at his own watch. It's time, he says.*

The two men hoist him to the door and out into the hall. They hold him up in the doorway. Downstairs, down the stairwell, many flights down, he can hear remnants of the everyday world. People asking for a licence, a special stamp, a signature. He can hear coughing and the scraping of chairs. The hinges of doors creak open and shut. Just at that moment an elderly woman comes past, supported at her elbows by two men. Her body hangs forward, she does not look up as she passes but she seems familiar to him. One side of her face bruised and swollen.

Her lip is split. He turns away, as if he has not seen. Then they take him back into the office. He is shaking hard.

Tell us, says the commanding officer, 5 September 1962? Where were you? What were you doing?

5 September 1962. So long ago. The professor's eyes are closed. He can no longer remember a life before this room.

The commanding officer consults a file. You were on a train to Piraeus. You were reading Avghí *on a train to Piraeus. You can hide nothing, the officer continues. We know everything. Your cell is destroyed. You are the last man left.*

Cell? The word comes.

The universities are full of Reds. The officer clicks his tongue: It's like this. The world is in two parts. The Free World and the Reds. We're all Americans now. He points proudly to his desk and the insignia of the American food aid programme. He points to the small stars and stripes flag on his cabinet. The Americans know everything. Who wants a Red Greece? They support us because we support democracy.

The professor keeps his mouth shut.

The commanding officer gets up and paces the room. Then he kneels down and comes in close. So close that the professor can see his eyes. What he sees there surprises him. They are the eyes of an ordinary man. A decent man with a family and a wife. A man who goes to church on Sundays. A man forced to do something he finds difficult, but necessary. He puts his hand on the professor's shoulder and for a brief moment it feels like a gesture of comfort. He gets up with effort. Then remembers his audience. He swings around and thumps the desk, reasserting himself. I'm a hunter. It's the family business. I've been hunting Reds for years. My father before me. Since the Civil War, he says. Governments come and go. We remain. If you don't talk or sign, it's prison and then an island camp. Then you'll come running.

The professor looks up.

Believe it. The stories after the war! Believe it — you all turn in the end. For the sake of your children and your children's children.

I have no children.

Don't lie to us.

The officer walks over and opens the shutters. He gently probes the soil of the basil pots on the window sill. Too dry, he says. He goes to the sink, fills a glass of water and pours the water in one pot and then the other. He fills another glass of water and comes back to sit on the desk.

Talk! he says in a strained voice, then nods to the small policeman.

The small policeman grabs the professor and drags him to the bench. The professor becomes the bench. He floats away. He becomes an ocean creature. Moving slowly over the ocean floor. He looks up at mouths and eyes moving. He cannot speak. He tries to keep thinking, naming. The name of the small platía near his apartment. All the períptero owners in the square. The xéni who returned to Australia. For him, it was never serious. With Irini, it is different. With Irini it has always been different. He hasn't seen her since the night of the coup. Inside himself, he says her name again. Irini, the woman he loves. Keep naming until you go under, that's what the old timers say. The names in his address book. The names he must protect. The names of his students. Phone numbers he knows by heart. Poems. Songs.

The commanding officer calls for a halt.

Then a smell of bleach and water and his head is held back. He wakes up after a short time or maybe a long time: cold, wet, covered in vomit.

The commanding officer moves to the washbasin. He looks at his watch. Enough. He takes a comb out of his back pocket. Runs it through the water and then through his hair. In the mirror he looks back at the man on the ground and feels a spasm of disgust or maybe pity. He has been doing this job for too long. Enough for one day, he says, and leaves the room.

Meanwhile the professor keeps rolling with the sea. With the waves. Under the waves.

I'm no terrorist, he says at one point. He doesn't know at what point.

Surrounded by clean-shaven men – military men – he resolves to grow a beard.

He goes deep inside and finds a trapdoor to his interior life. He can hide under rocks, under waves, deep on the ocean floor. In his mind he's anywhere he wants to be. He is a child on the island of his grandparents. He can see the Portara glowing on the headland and the first girl he ever kissed there. He goes over every job he has ever done and every woman he has ever been with. He tests the reaches of himself.

If I ever get out of here my life will be very different. Away from politics and history. Away from words.

He remembers his joyful times on the island as a boy. Those times become very important. The land and the sea and the air; that's all he can think about.

He could give one name or another. He could give a million names and it would bring such sweet relief – as cigarettes are lit and his arms are held down and part of him is burnt away forever.

The Island

4

A woman was here asking for you, said Stefanos as he wiped the table and placed the small coffee cup next to the glass of water. He knew exactly what Andreas wanted without having to ask. Always the same, for all these years: *Ellinikó, dipló, métrio.*

What kind of woman? Andreas looked up from his book. He steadied himself, felt a clench round the heart. Over the years he hoped that every woman would be Irini. Long after news of her disappearance reached him. Long after there was anything to hope for.

Not old. Not young.

Pretty? Andreas forced a laugh, but his friend looked serious as he shifted back behind the bar.

She looked familiar, said Stefanos and shrugged, looking away.

Familiar?

Nai.

Andreas caught something in his tone. Stefanos looked around the tables. How to alert his friend? The kafé was full of people they both knew. People from the *Hóra*, the town. People from the village. Over the years they'd discussed the possibility. The likelihood of the child turning up, fully grown. They'd argued about it – Stefanos was a family man while Andreas was an eternal *kamáki* with no idea of family. They'd made a joke of it. They'd even placed bets on it. Stefanos paused, then added, She's a *xéni*.

A *xéni*? Andreas tensed, then forced himself to relax. There were plenty of foreigners on the island. He was known as a handyman. Perhaps someone needed repairs.

I Germanída?

I Anglída. English, said Stefanos. She speaks English.

From where?

She left quickly, said Stefanos, looking away. This wasn't quite true and they both knew it. Trying to convey everything through his expression, his lowered voice. Stefanos shrugged. Perhaps I made a mistake, he thought. *Perhaps.* But those eyes. It must be her. He didn't mention her boy child. She speaks English, he repeated. She will come tomorrow. At eleven. I told her you would be here.

Andreas had enjoyed his second coffee at his friend's bar for many years. Since when it was only a *kafenío*, further down in the *Kástro*, full of men playing *távli* and drinking ouzo. Before the tourists and the wealthy Athenians had come. Before it became 'To Steki'; before the chrome bar fittings and the soft lights, long before the comfortable seats and the menu in many languages.

What does she want? Andreas was suddenly on high alert, that old reflex. All that time waiting for the knock at the door, waiting at a dark window with a suitcase packed, listening for feet on the stairs. All the old suspicions flushed his system like a drug.

Just to see you. Nothing more.

You didn't tell my address?

Tomorrow at eleven. You will meet with her. Again he gave Andreas a serious look. He wiped down the counter, then smiled, leant over and whispered:

Our bet was in drachmas. Now, *re maláka*, it's euros.

*

The next day Andreas got up at dawn and had his first coffee. He went to tend the goats and the chickens. To feed his dog. To inspect the olive trees and cut the vines right back. These days he was an early riser. When he was young he would stay up all night and sleep late. Work in the afternoons. His old life had a completely different rhythm. A city rhythm. Here on the island he liked the mornings best – to be awake before everyone else, before the day really began. To feel as if he were the only man in the world. To feel free.

At times he would wake in a sweat, thinking that everything had been taken away. All the old pains would flame through. As if his wrists were still tied, the fingers broken and bars still on the windows. As if the only living thing was the moon, slanting the floor.

He had that feeling now. The soles of his feet started to ache. His neck hurt as if being held down.

As the sun moved higher in the sky he became more and more agitated. He slapped at his donkey and pushed himself hard, without a break, enacting a penance. As if he still believed in such things from his childhood – still waiting for the *Papás* to absolve

73

him. He went hours without a cigarette or a break but when he stopped he'd made his decision. He didn't want to meet this *xéni* in a public place, in front of his friends or in front of people from the village who would talk. Marsoula had warned him that this might happen. Stefanos had always known that this would come. He went out to the telephone box at the end of the path, near the bus stop. He looked at his wristwatch. It was 10.30. He put in his phone card and dialled the kafé.

Tell her I'm not coming, he said to Stefanos. Tell her I've gone away.

But already she's here. His friend dropped his voice. She's waiting for you.

Merde. Andrea always swore in French. An old reflex, from his life before. He struck the side of the telephone.

It's too late, said Stefanos. Then, apologetically: I gave your address.

You have the big mouth, said Andreas.

It is better this way, said Stefanos. You must meet her.

Andreas sighed. Tell her to come later. At two. I'm working now. To himself, he murmured, *Panaghía mou. Theé mou.* Help me.

*

She approached the village on a bicycle borrowed from the hotel, cycling away from the town. The Portara glowed out on the headland, white in the winter sun. She felt it framing her own feelings. This birth father had not wanted to see her. She'd

74

arrived early and she could tell from the bar owner's insistence, his hushed voice on the telephone, that Andreas had not wanted to meet her. Catherine had been right. *Not a person to rely on.* The man, Stefanos, had looked at her with pity as he scrawled a small map on a paper napkin and handed it over. You will find him there, he said. At two.

Two o'clock?

He's working now. The man shrugged.

Oh no, she thought. *I'll have to go back and explain all this to Alex. Rearrange the afternoon.*

She'd slept badly. All night she'd fretted about what to do with her son. She'd fretted about meeting her birth father. In the end, she decided to leave Alex with the family who ran the hotel. They had a girl about his age. He'd been shy at first but then he'd joined in their games, unable to resist the exuberant child and her boy cousins. Still, he wasn't happy to be left behind. When Lena told him she had to go alone he'd tantrumed around their small room. Thrown his Nintendo. Refused to brush his teeth after breakfast.

It's the first time, she said. I have to go by myself.

But why?

Because I have to. She couldn't think of anything else to say. Then she added: It will be easier. *Because it will be too much for me and perhaps too much for all of us.* She left the last part unsaid. And then to come back from the kafé so soon! Of course the kid was confused. He looked so hopeful when he saw her return. I have to go later, she said. There was a mix-up.

Can I come?

You know you can't.

She didn't want Alex to see her so raw. So eager to be set up for hurt or rejection. To see his mother as she truly was – not much more than a child herself. She needed to go alone. Eventually she'd left him again at the hotel, after all the pleading and the tears, playing happily with the little girl out in the courtyard. I'll be back soon, she said. We can go up to the Portara at sunset. Alex nodded and she kissed the top of his head. As Lena was leaving, the girl's uncle arrived on a small motorbike. He had lengths of plastic tubing at his feet and wooden slats attached to the back seat by rope. He was about to make *tsípouro*, he called out, would the children like to see?

What's *tsípouro*? asked Alex

The man explained that it was a drink, a drink for grown-up men.

Alex, entranced by the barrel, the tubing, the motorbike, by the man's warmth and good humour, said that yes, he would like to see. Just then the owner of the hotel, the girl's mother, came to reassure Lena that they would all make *tsípouro* with her brother. The children were safe with them, not to worry. Lena took her chance to say goodbye. She told them she'd be back before sunset. A couple of hours at the most, she thought.

They'd been on the island for a few days before Lena had worked up the nerve to go looking. She'd wanted to get the feel of the place. Each day she walked down the steps from the hotel and along the *paralía* with Alex. They liked to pause along the seafront, looking out at the small church in the harbour, at the

76

old fishermen darning nets or sitting in kafés. Most of the harbour restaurants were shut and there were few tourists around.
The Christmas lights were still up. She knew that they were
objects of curiosity – a *xéni* with her son, here out of season. She
scanned the faces of the older men, wondering if one of them
was her father. On their way back to the hotel one evening they
took a detour deep into the *Kástro*, the old Venetian quarter
behind their hotel. It was dark and the lanes wound through small
arches and the street lamps made little impact. It was a medieval
scene of retreating shadows. Eventually, she saw a woman filling
a water container at a public tap and showed her the name and
address on the paper from Athens. This *kafenío* didn't exist anymore, the woman said, but Stefano has a new place. 'To Steki'.
Further down. Around from the book store that is no longer
open. You could try there.

She'd felt self-conscious walking in with Alex. There were
only men at the tables, drinking coffee, talking politics, playing
távli. There was a television on a news loop in the corner. The
conservative Prime Minister was under fire for corruption –
shady land deals with Mount Athos. His Nea Dimokratia government was trailing in the polls. All around there was talk of a
snap election and that the opposition PASOK would win. There
was something timeless about the scene, about the faces of the
men. It reminded her of the Greek places along Sydney Road.
Although it had cream sofas and soft lighting it was still a *kafenío*.
The clientele hadn't changed. The owner made a fuss of Alex
and then quizzed her, not unkindly, about where she was from

and why she wanted to meet his old friend. He'd given Alex a sweet. Distant relatives, she said. Just travelling through. *Relatives?* He looked sceptical. She realized that this was because he *knew* exactly who she was. The recognition shocked her. To have a physical resemblance with someone she'd never met, enough that a stranger would know. She gripped the piece of paper in her hand and had a sudden desire to pull back, get on the next boat and sail for somewhere else.

But she was here, now, on this road, on her bicycle. *I am going to meet my father.* She kept repeating it to herself, as if in repetition it would sink in, become true. Like a muscle worked over and over, a body memory. The road became less even, more winding and full of potholes and cracks, patched in places with fresh black tar. As it dipped down into the village, bamboo fringed the road and divided the farms from each other, forming wind breaks. Great stalks of agave, trees in their own right, reached up. A huge trunk of agave had fallen across the road and she had to cycle round it. The sun was warm at her back but a cool wind bit her face. At the bus stop, just past the sign to the village, she got off the bike. This was where the man, Stefanos, had told her to wait. She tried to read a photocopied sheet stapled to an electricity pylon. It showed an animal with its throat cut. She couldn't make out the animal, but as she read, she realized it was about dogs. About the murder of dogs. In this village and in neighbouring villages. Her reading in Greek still wasn't good, she was very slow, mouthing out the words to herself, trying to understand. In the field opposite, a man walked behind a donkey, slapping its flanks, ensuring the hoe ploughed straight. She stopped to watch, to marvel over this ancient way of doing things. Further along, in an adjacent field, a man with a tractor was doing exactly the same work.

She wondered which man she was supposed to meet.

*

It was just after two. The man with the plough frowned when he saw her, tethered his donkey and walked to the edge of the field. He called out, *Welcome,* in English but the greeting was without warmth. He was a slight man with a neat beard. Not much taller than herself. A tanned face under a blue cap. They shook hands formally. His shirtsleeves were rolled to the elbow. She saw that his hands were scarred and burn marks tracked up his forearms. His grip was strong and she winced a little. She had a band-aid on her right palm where the cuts from the stolen badge were slow to heal.

My name is Andreas, he said, pulling down his shirtsleeves.

I'm Lena. She was sweating. Words deserted her – Greek, English – everything she'd prepared. She tried to speak again.

He saw the plaster. Your hand is sore?

Den pirázi, she said. No matter. Her self-inflicted wounds.

She pushed up her sunglasses and he studied her face. It came as shock to see himself there. *The eyes.* It was true then, he thought to himself. After all this time, the girl. Marsoula had warned him. Stefanos had been right. The child had come here. The grown-up child.

79

I know who you are, he cut her off. Then in Greek and English, *Éla*. Come.

He walked quickly. He had to be seventy, but to Lena he looked at least a decade younger. He was lean and tanned and fit. Accustomed to hard physical work. He moved beautifully. A loose, easy walk, long-limbed. The walk of a much taller man, she thought.

She followed him up the steep path to the house. She remembered the word for path and repeated it silently to herself. *To dromáki*. It led off the main road edging the village, away from the fields. It was only wide enough for a small car or a donkey. The houses along it were all fairly new, built in the Cycladic style familiar from postcards. The whitewashed cubes, blue shutters, marble floors. Wooden pergolas over the balconies. Whether a house was one hundred years old or newly done, it was simple – blue and white – a reflection of the sky and the sea. Most houses had a small garden or courtyard in front. He led her to a compact two-storey house at the corner of the path. The house was built right into the side of the mountain. Bougainvillea branches roped across the pergola, mixing with the vines. In summer it would be red or pink, she thought, but now it was too early; it was all thorns. Jasmine, not yet flowering, trailed the wooden posts at the front. A huge rubber tree and a monkey puzzle tree dwarfed the triangle of garden, giving shade to the front of the house. They climbed up the steps, past geraniums opening early in olive oil tins, past a small bedroom with its shutters slightly ajar. Tsssk! Andreas checked inside the shutters. The wild cats! he said. Then on up to the first-floor balcony. A pot of basil by the window sill. He pushed the blue door open, drew back the curtain and urged her through.

It was dark and close inside. It smelt of wood smoke. There was a fireplace in one corner. A large black pot simmered on the stove. He lifted the lid and stirred the contents. There was another black pot next to it. A sieve, a wire grill and a frying pan were suspended on hooks from the wall and a pocket knife lay open on the marble worktop. A small wooden mortar and pestle stood next to the stove. There was the scent of rosemary, thyme and fennel.

His house was austere by Greek standards and this is what struck her. There were no heavy furnishings or curtains; no wall hangings or ornate cushions. No photographs of family on the walls. No ornaments of any kind. There was a sofa and a small wooden table and a kilim on the floor.

His kitchen and sitting room were one space. He moved to the back of the kitchen, checked the pots on the stove then pushed aside a door curtain to a book-heaped study and opened a small window, buffeting the room with a cold wind. The *Voriás*, he said, but too cold now, he shut the window again and came out of the study. *Pagoménos*, he said, and shivered. Like ice. He wasn't able to look at her. He was all restless movement. She stood stock still in the doorway.

When the wind comes from the north, in summer, it is cool, it is good. When it comes from the south – the hot wind – the *Notiás* – it's trouble! He muttered all this to himself in Greek and

English and then noticed that she was still standing in the door-way. *Éla!* he said. Come.

Sit! he said. He shook out a cushion. Exchanged one cushion for another. Motioned her to sit.

He moved deftly around the kitchen. He couldn't stop moving. He set an empty water jug and two glasses on a side table. For the first time he turned to face her properly and smiled a nervous smile.

Edáksi. Dáksi. OK?

OK. She smiled nervously back.

He took a deep breath. Stood up straight, one hand on a cup-board, steadying himself to face her. He addressed her in English, coolly: So. The daughter.

She looked over at him, startled.

Then in that manner which seemed so abrupt and untrans-latable from Greek to English, he said suddenly: What do you want?

She didn't know by his tone whether he was referring to food or drink or to the reason for her visit. She straightened up, was about to speak, to tell him why she was here, but then he frowned and answered the question himself.

First, of course, *neró*. Water.

He lifted a large plastic bottle from the floor and filled the jug and poured her a glass and one for himself. I get it from the well, he said. Do not drink from the house tap, he cautioned. The *Dímos*, the council, put *hloríni* in the water. Is no good for drinking.

Then, looking around his small kitchen, he put his hand to the back of his head and muttered again to himself. He returned to the stove. Lifted the lids off the pots. Almost ready, he said.

You didn't have to cook, she said.

He gave her a strange look. I always cook, he said. Is nothing special.

Oh.

You do not like the Greek food?

No. It's just that ...

Then eat, he said.

She didn't know what to make of it; to make of him. She hadn't expected a meal and she wasn't hungry. He kept opening and closing cupboards; taking out plates and plastic tubs of all sizes. He reached down into a cupboard and drew handfuls of unshelled almonds from a hessian sack. As he bent to the sack, his shirt lifted a little and she saw scars on his lower spine.

He put the almonds on a plate. These are from outside, he said, gesturing to the almond trees in the fields. *Dikó mou*. He added in English again, Mine.

She nodded. I speak a little Greek, she said. No need to translate.

You know Greek? He laughed, surprised, cracked his knuckles and seemed to relax a little. Bravo. Greek is difficult. French is my other language. He inclined his head. I know some English but I read better than I speak.

I speak better than I read. She said this in Greek and then added: But I make many mistakes.

83

We learn with the mistakes, he said in English. We will speak *misó-misó*? Half and half?

OK, she said.

He kept assembling food on plates. Anchovies. Cucumber. Tomatoes. He was fully and deeply involved in what he was doing. The cutting of cheese. The arrangement of almonds. The cutting of the apple – vertically, the correct way – she noticed. The way she always forgot. The slicing of the apple and the placement of toothpicks in each slice. The slow care he took with everything. It was only with dance that she paid such attention. In every other area of her life she was all over the place. When excited she was still prone to dropping things, cutting herself, bruising herself. She wasn't much of a cook. In that she took after her mother. Her mind ran on. These past months, what had they eaten? What had she fed Alex? Since Johnny's funeral, since her operation – sandwiches, eggs, Heinz tomato soup. Plates in aluminium foil left by friends at the back door.

Well, he said. *I kóri.* He said it in Greek this time – the daughter – interrupting her thoughts. He said the words as if they were a private joke. We move *ékso*?

As they moved to the balcony, she calculated how long she should stay, when she should get back to Alex. It was around three o'clock and the winter sun hung low in the sky. It would be dark by five. The pergola was covered with a tough tangle of vines, recently pruned. He set the food on a wooden table with a marble top. Several plastic chairs ranged around it. He smoothed a plastic cloth over the marble. He urged her to sit and when all the plates and trays were brought through, including the pots from the stove, he sat down. He breathed in deeply.

It was a sheltered spot. The huge leaves of the rubber trees lifted in the wind, making a gamelan sound. And then she was off: the first trip she'd taken to Bali. Gamelan and incense and clove cigarettes. The fire dance in Ubud, she remembered that. No matter that it was for tourists. No matter that they performed seven nights a week. The dancers were good, some were excellent. Johnny and her mother had been with them. Johnny always remembered places by the meals they'd had. He had a culinary memory. Whereas her memory was – what, exactly? If she thought hard she could remember how people gestured, how they walked. The line of them.

Andreas said again that she should eat.

A feast! she said. Then in Greek, *Megálo trapézi.*

He grinned and she could see a couple of teeth missing at the back. Big table! he translated. Your Greek is good!

Thank you. She felt her face flush. Her Greek was limited but she was glad it pleased him.

Kalí óreksi, he said. Bon appétit. How they say in English?

She paused. Well, we don't. Not exactly.

Ah, yes! I remember. The English have no time for food. It is quick. It is gone. Then they drink.

She laughed, uncertainly. The English? But I'm Australian.

The same, he said. Then saw the look on her face. Same words, he checked himself. The English – no word for good eating. No time for food. He picked up his fork. Eat!

She did as she was told and put some olives on her plate. He'd made *mavromátika* – black-eyed beans with tomato, and in the other pot he'd made *spanakórizo* – spinach with rice. He tested the rice. Too hot, he said. Wait! He pointed to the cheese instead.

Graviéra cheese. From this island. You are too thin, he said. You must eat. He tore off a piece of bread and handed it to her. She felt self-conscious as he watched her eat. He took sips of water and twisted small pieces from his bread. He poured her a glass of wine from a metal pitcher. Asked if she wanted any ice.

No ice, she said.

Yeía mas. To us, he said, but without enthusiasm.

Yeía mas! she said, raising her glass. She took a sip. The wine was pale, rose-coloured, with a sherry tang.

You like it? *Dikó mou*, he said. Mine. From my grapes.

You make everything?

Not everything. But a lot. A lot. He bent his head to his plate.

It's your farm?

Now, yes. I bought it. My own *horáfi*. There was a silence and then he urged her to taste the spinach and rice. The black beans. Is cooler now, he said. Hot food is not good. Is very bad. He paused. Every Greek knows this.

Nóstimo, she said. Delicious, she murmured in English, even though she liked her food hot. She had a memory of that first trip to Athens. On every counter in every taverna – food cooling in trays. You ordered and waited for it to cool.

She pushed the lukewarm rice around the plate and repeated, Delicious.

The air was fraught between them.

She put down her fork. I have some questions, she said.

And I must warn you, he said in Greek, putting his own fork down. Perhaps no answers.

Then he picked up his fork again to put rice and spinach on his plate. Took a few mouthfuls and stopped. Reached over for a slice of cheese. He drew a pack of cigarettes from his pocket and then a lighter and put both on the table between them.

Lena looked hungrily at the cigarettes. She thought of the stolen packet in her bag, three-quarters full. She could ration herself. She could be disciplined. She could wait until she was alone. Andreas also looked at the cigarettes on the table. Patted them as if for reassurance, for later, and returned to his food. Some kind of smoker's tic. She recognized the gesture. And now that the cigarettes were there between them she found it hard to think of anything else.

Your mother speaks bad of me. I know. She has nothing good to say. How can it be different? His hand moved to the cigarettes. I understand.

Lena wanted to say, *You have no idea*. Instead, she said, You understand?

He smiled. Yes. He paused and smiled again. But she is wrong.

On her mother's behalf she wanted to protest, but he put up a hand to stay her.

He cleared his throat: This man now and the man who knew your mother are two different things.

Despite herself, she said, You're sure?

Ax! I left you all these years as if I hadn't a daughter. But I knew of you. Of course. He looked at her quickly, to see how she would take this and continued. She sent me a letter. But I was young. It was a different time. A hard time. His voice was suddenly forced and sharp at the edges. I'm not the good father. I don't understand family. He leant back in his chair and sighed. What do you want from me?

After this outburst she kept silent for a while. She, too, leant back in her chair.

I don't know, she said simply. What could she tell him without seeming lost? Without seeming ridiculous? She reached for her wine glass.

Po, po, pó, he said sadly, leaning forward and extracting a cigarette. You are here to be disappointed.

Lena sat there, forcing small bites of lukewarm food into her mouth, food that she didn't want. What she wanted was a cigarette. Inside herself she was curled up into a small ball. Inside herself she was a child and she wanted to get away.

Greece. What do you think of Greece? he asked awkwardly, changing the subject.

I like Greece, she said. I love it.

The first visit?

No.

You came before? He clearly hadn't expected this. He raised his eyebrows. Took a deep inhale.

I was in Athens, many years ago. I stayed for ten days.

And you didn't come here? His tone suspicious.

No. It wasn't the right time.

He paused. Tried to gauge her; how far to push. And *now* is the right time?

Maybe.

And you *love* it here? He was suddenly on the attack. What does that mean? You love the politics? You love that we are the poor man of Europe? Pah! All foreigners they come for the sun, for the sea, but understand nothing.

Where I come from, she shot back, we have sun and sea.

Of course. His voice sarcastic. You come for the *culture*.

Not culture-starved, either.

Ax! Australia is so new, he said.

Australia is so old. To a colonial mentality, it's new ...

He sat back, nodded to himself. Looked at her with approval. Bravo! The colonial mentality! He smiled. You're clever.

I know. She matched his tone. But I don't need to be tested.

She was tired. He knew nothing about her and it was tedious, she thought. Having to prove her intelligence. With a certain kind of man it was always the same, having to prove herself in this way. She was too old for this sort of conversation.

You are Right, you are Left?

More Left than Right, she said. I guess.

You *guess*? You don't *know*?

Politics isn't really my thing.

Edáksi, OK, he said impatiently and tapped out another cigarette. OK. But the colonial mentality. This is good. Smart! He then gave her a short lecture on the history of Australia, the long history of Aboriginal people, the abuses of the British, as if she knew nothing. She listened politely, nodded and smiled in all the right places. Not for the first time she thought to herself, *Women are too polite. I'm too polite.* She swallowed more wine, looked longingly at the cigarettes and choked back her annoyance.

Well, she conceded, an unaccustomed edge to her own voice. You know some history. *He's bringing out the worst in me,* she thought.

I was the Professor of Ottoman History. It's my specialism.

You were a professor?

He nodded. At the University of Athens.

So, she decided to ask because it seemed to interest him. Are you Left or Right?

Left, he said emphatically. They thought I was the communist . . .

And now?

Today? Pah! I'm away from all politics.

It seemed to her that this wasn't actually the case, but they stayed quiet for a while. She still didn't know what to make of him. He smoked cigarettes and refilled her water. He pointed to her small empty wine glass.

Lígo akóma? he asked, and without waiting for an answer went inside to get more wine.

When he came back, she tried to resume the conversation. Greece has changed a lot, she said. From nearly twenty years ago. From what I remembered. The airport. Plaka. The air, even.

Back then, the *néfos* was so bad over Athens. We'd wash our white T-shirts, hang them to dry on the balcony – they'd be yellow by morning . . . She trailed off. She felt headachy and small in his company.

Many changes, he agreed. Some good. Some bad. Then abruptly, What is your work?

I'm a dancer. Then she corrected herself. A dance teacher.

A dancer? He took in her slight frame, almost boyish. No chest to speak of. Long defined limbs. A dancer, he repeated. From what he remembered of her mother, there was little resemblance. He had to admit that she looked Greek. He had to admit, despite himself, that she looked like him.

You look like a dancer, he said. But – too thin! You are sick?

She felt pleased when he said she looked like a dancer. My vanity's still intact, she thought. The only thing intact.

I'm OK, she said. Although she wasn't OK, not at all. She closed around herself and her hurts. I eat. I'm fine. Trying to heal up from the operation. But she wasn't about to tell him that.

You do the Greek dancing?

No, she responded seriously. Too seriously. Contemporary dance.

Oh.

She could see he didn't understand.

How old when you started?

From young, she said in Greek. I trained, I toured. Then. She didn't have the words to describe the end of her dancing career. To have no energy for dancing. To exist on 500 calories a day. An apple and a Diet Coke. Amphetamines and cigarettes. To make yourself sick to the point where the thing you most love is the thing you can't do any more.

He raised his eyebrows, looked puzzled.

I took time out from my dancing.

And then?

I became a teacher, she said and then hesitated. I haven't danced in a long while. And I'm getting older. It's been a hard year, she said, without looking up. She was sick of words. She felt unable to articulate anything. She had a sudden desire to get up and move in the old way. To fully inhabit the moment; to lose herself. To show how she truly felt. A woman on a stage with one shoe. A woman on a stage by herself, trying to find her way back.

These days, I teach. She went on, I teach children at a primary school.

You like this work?

I like it. She paused. Mostly. It fulfilled a part of herself. She loved the kids. At least he's asking questions, she thought, though it felt more like an interrogation. At least he's not lecturing me.

You like it as much as the dancing?

For me, dancing was different, she said, without hesitation, without smiling. Dancing was life.

*

He was silent for a while and then resumed his previous topic. It was a conversation of twists and turns.

Greece has changed, he said. In the old days, everyone made everything. The land was all. Then the 1980s! He spread his scarred hands on the table and leaned towards her to make his point. EU money. The easy way to spend it is roads. Roads and cars. People lose relation to the land. They lose respect for it.

On my way here, she said, determined to keep the conversation going, I passed a field – a rubbish dump. Fridges and plastic bags and machine parts . . .

But we have recycling, he interrupted, obliged to defend Greece. On the island, this past six months . . .

But who empties the bins? she said. Where does it all go? *And why are we fixating on rubbish?*

Lipón. My parents' generation were different. We were different. They lacked basic things. They threw nothing away. They had nothing. No refrigerator. No telephone. No car or television. Now, this generation have *ola*, they have all. But at what cost? Everyone in debt. He shook his head. Today, everyone has everything. They want only the new. They throw out the old. Into the fields. Into the streets . . .

But as a communist, she said, an edge to her voice that was her mother, an edge that she didn't like, don't you want everyone to have everything? She'd once had a relationship with a communist. He was self-involved and infantile, she remembered. Always at meetings. Always selling newspapers at Flinders Street station. Always sleeping around because monogamy was bourgeois. But when she'd had an affair he fell to bits. She understood too well the gap between theory and practice.

Suspected communist, he corrected. He lit a cigarette and slit his eyes at her through the blue smoke. You are here how long?

Three days. She said the first thing that came to mind. She had no idea how long they'd stay. But at the moment, in the middle of this conversation, three days seemed long enough.

Only? She thought she saw a flicker of something. Relief? Disappointment? Something passed across his face, some tightening around the mouth, around the eyes.

In three days, what can you know?

She shrugged. Where should we start?

From the beginning, he said, tapping out his cigarette.

*

He didn't start from the beginning. In fact, when she thought about it later, he avoided getting started altogether.

More wine? He indicated her empty glass and before she could say anything he went into the kitchen and got more wine. He refilled her glass.

She looked at her watch. She would have to go soon.

This wine – he held up the glass – this is *kaloksiméroto to krasí*. This means – good wine for staying up until dawn. He tapped his forehead. No headache. I made it myself. *Edáksi?* OK?

It's good wine, she said. But I must go soon. Aware that she should stop drinking. She craved a cigarette.

He clinked glasses with her. *Yeía mas*, he said sadly. To us.

She put down her glass. Actually, Andreas, what I want is a cigarette. She spoke in Greek and was happy to be so direct. All the evasions and circumlocutions of English left behind. And then I really have to go.

You smoke? His tone was approving.

I used to smoke. I gave up two months ago. She didn't mention that she'd been forced to give up, that she'd been in hospital. I started again on the ferry.

As a Greek, he said, it's your patriotic duty. He wasn't joking. He pushed the packet of cigarettes towards her.

As an Australian, I'll remember that. She lit the cigarette, glad of the distraction. Glad to have something to occupy her hands other than a glass. Jesus, she thought. What was she doing? Her son disapproved and her stepfather had died of lung cancer. Again the nicotine hit her right between the eyes.

You are alone? From nowhere, it seemed, he came out with the question. No husband? He'd been wondering about this. Had presumed it, in fact. *No husband.* She seemed ill and adrift and he knew nothing about her. She had one of those faces which showed every passing emotion. *He knew nothing about her.* A deliberate policy. For years, the only policy. Every time Marsoula had tried to talk to him about it he'd turned away. And now, here she was, this daughter. It was harder to turn away when she was right in front of him. He repeated, You are not married?

No, she said.

He lit another cigarette and waited for her to continue.

She tapped at her cigarette. I've never been married, she said. Not formally. She inhaled deeply then exhaled. I've lived with people. I've loved people. I never married. It wasn't a big deal.

You didn't marry? You were the hippy?

No. *Not a hippy.* She didn't know whether to be annoyed or amused. She pulled at a rent in the plastic tablecloth.

Why you didn't marry?

Now she was annoyed.

Marriage isn't the be-all and end-all, she said. A good relationship makes people happy. Not marriage, as such. She pulled again at the run in the tablecloth. She didn't know how to explain. How when she was small, she would sit in the bath with a flannel over her face and breathe in deep and slide under the water and – she remembers it clearly, she was eleven years old when the thought first came – *this is marriage and children* – a trapped, underwater feeling.

She paused. Did you ever marry?

No, he said.

Well, then.

For women, is different.

For you, maybe.

I'm sorry, said Andreas.

That I'm not married? It was hard to keep her tone even.

No. He looked away and then surprised her by saying, For everything.

She couldn't work out whether he was talking about his life or her own.

Well. She raised her wine glass. It was her turn to change tack, to surprise him. Actually, I have a son, she said. She checked her watch again. And I must be getting back to him.

Andreas swivelled around. A son?

She had a small photograph in her wallet of Alex doing a back flip. He's bigger now, but I love this photo. She showed it to Andreas. He has fair hair and brown eyes, she said.

Andreas brought the photo up close to his face and then held it further away. His glasses were in the next room. The photograph was in black and white. He couldn't make out the child's face but he noted the hair and the skin. Marsoula must have known all of this. She'd protected him from it for years.

He looks Greek?

Lena smiled. I guess so, yes. A fair Greek, she said. His father was Scottish.

Andreas smiled, a little bemused. Then narrowed his eyes. Where is he now?

The father?

The child, said Andreas.

He's in town, in the *Hóra*. I left him at the hotel.

Andreas looked at the photo again. *Ómorfos,* he said. Handsome. She could see that he was trying to take it in. *A grandson*, he said and touched the photograph.

You left him? Andreas wasn't happy. She could see it in his face. You should have brought him here.

You're kidding me. Lena pushed back in her chair.

Andreas gave her a blank look. *Den katalavéno.*

It's *argó*, she said. It means, are you joking? She repeated in Greek: *Pláka mou kánis.*

He drew himself up in his seat. I'm his grandfather.

I had to meet you first. How did I know what to expect?

And now you know.

Yes, she said, taking the old Zippo lighter from her bag and playing with the lid. I sure do. They stared at each other over the chasm of the table and she had a feeling that he was about to say something she didn't want to hear.

You know your boy, at least. Andreas took a final drag of his cigarette, turning away. This is something. But for me, is different. I never knew you. I never wanted you. He ground his cigarette butt into the ashtray. Took another from the packet.

She reeled at this. Felt rubbed raw. As if she'd been expelled from the birth canal into a bright and brittle world. He got up suddenly to go to the kitchen. When he came back, his eyes were wet. He sat down heavily at the table and leant across.

Are you here to find a father?

I had a father. She saw him flinch. My stepfather. He died a few months ago. I'm here to have a break.

From loneliness?

Who says I'm lonely?

She sat there with dry eyes. Tapped out another cigarette. She used to be so disciplined. Now she'd smoked several cigarettes in a row. Her chest was heavy and her throat was sore. Her abdomen ached around the scar. She was aware that she'd had too much to drink.

This will be a long three days, she thought to herself.

*

She sipped at her wine then looked at her watch. I must go. I have to get back to Alex. I told him I'd only be away a short time. She didn't know whether she should suggest another meeting.

He clicked his tongue, raised his chin. Your mother kept contact with Marsoula.

Marsoula? You're kidding me.

This time he understood the expression. My sister.

My mother said she lost contact.

They were friends. They are still friends.

Where does Marsoula live?

In the mountains.

Does she know I'm here?

She thought you would come. Your mother wrote to her. Marsoula tried to warn me.

Warn you?

He shrugged. She knows my character.

We should see her. Lena was adamant.

Maybe.

You don't want us to meet?

It's just that . . . *sigá, sigá*. Slowly, slowly.

Lena was suddenly impatient. I'm only here for a short time.

He hesitated. She lives in Apeira. In the mountains. He started shredding a paper napkin between his fingers.

What's wrong, Andreas?

I have a daughter. He pointed to her. A grown woman. He put down the shredded napkin. Reached for the lighter. And now a grandson!

Nothing to be ashamed of.

Perhaps. He looked up, smiled a slow smile.

They sat in silence as the sun lowered in the sky over the hills towards Paros. A great red eye of a sun, watching them.

You want coffee? I have filter.

No, I . . .

Before she could answer he went back inside and put a coffee machine on the electric stove. She looked again at her watch. She had to go. He came out with a jar full of sticky spoon sweet – lemon – also from his trees, he said.

She took one sip of her coffee, glanced at the spoon sweet and then stood up. I'm sorry, she said. I really have to go.

Andreas also stood up. He cleared his throat. He looked out past the rubber tree into the distance. Tomorrow, maybe, we could go to Apeira. I could take you to Marsoula.

Tomorrow?

You have the plans for tomorrow?

No. No. But . . . *sigá, sigá?*

He smiled and shrugged. You are here only for the few days . . .

We don't have any plans, she said quickly. I'd like to meet Marsoula. She wanted to say: *You were the only plan. You are the only reason I'm here.* But she stopped herself.

Kalá. I will meet you in the morning.

What time?

Same as today.

She checked. Two o'clock in the afternoon.

In Greece, it is morning. After five is afternoon.

OK, she said and smiled to herself. Two o'clock in the morning.

She smoothed down her skirt. Extended a hand. She felt too complicated to embrace him and a little high from the cigarettes and the wine.

Thank you, she said, aware that she was being very formal. Aware that she was taking her cue from him. In Greek she said, *Hárika.* Pleased to meet you.

He also stood up and gave a slight bow, grasped her hand and shook it very formally. She wasn't sure whether he was making fun of her or not.

Well, she said. Tomorrow. Shall we meet here?

No. I will come for you in my car.

She gave him the name of her hotel.

In the *Kástro*?

Nai, she said.

So you must wait on the *paralía*.

Of course, she said, knowing that the lanes of the *Kástro* could not take cars. Thank you for the meal.

He nodded and said brusquely, *Típota.* It's nothing. And then, *Yeía sou,* seeming to dismiss her, turning his attention to the dishes on the table, stacking the plates and pushing back through the curtain and into the house. She walked downstairs, holding on to the edge of the wall for support. The solar lights in the garden gave a weak glow. She picked up her bicycle and was about to ride off when he came onto the balcony again and called out: You will bring the boy?

I'll bring the boy, she said and then pedalled off without looking back, although her instinct was to wave, to call goodbye. She realized how much she'd had to drink only when she stood up, only when she started to pedal.

He stood there watching her freewheel unsteadily down the hill. He stood there with a dishcloth in his hands, alone there in the growing dark, looking out over the sea towards Paros. He stood there for some time, not knowing what to think, and then pushed back through the curtain and the night closed in around him.

5

They waited for Andreas out on the *paralía* the next afternoon.
After ten minutes, Alex grew restless. He ran over to see an old
man with an octopus, watching the man dash it again and again
against the steps of the port. At half past two Lena was giving up
when she saw a sand-coloured Deux Chevaux sputter along the
harbour road. She called Alex over. He was transfixed by a row
of translucent squid hanging outside a *kafenío*.

Is that him? Alex yelled back, pointing to the car. He was
bored, waiting for this person.

I think so, said Lena.

Earlier that morning, Lena had woken with a headache. She
felt ill. From the cigarettes, from the wine, from the stress of
meeting Andreas. Since the operation, she often had headaches.
At 5 a.m. she'd taken her last two Paracetamol. At the sight of the
car her head started to throb again.

Andreas parked at right angles to the curb. He kept the engine
on idle. His old exhaust billowed black into the street. Cars and
motorcycles beeped and edged around him.

Quick, he called through the open window. *Éla, páme!*

Alex – this is Andreas, she said as Alex clambered over the front seat.

Andreas turned around. Hello, he said stiffly in English and held out his hand.

Hello, said Alex and shook hands.

A truck beeped behind him and Andreas yelled something to the driver and put the car in gear. They jerked forward with the handbrake on.

All is *edáksi*? Andreas asked. She looked paler than yesterday. Despite himself, he felt a concern for her.

I thought we said two o'clock.

He snorted. The English. Always *stin óra*. Always on time. For us, is not so important.

It's hard with a child, she said. To wait so long . . .

He didn't answer.

She rubbed her temples and searched once more in her hand-bag for tablets she knew she didn't have. I'm sorry. I need to go to the chemist, she said. I've got a headache.

From my best wine?

She smiled. Yes and no.

Over there – he pointed to the *períptero* further along the main road. He slowed down.

Paracetamol from the kiosk?

Of course. A few drachmas, only.

He pulled up and handed her some change. Ask the man for Depon and water.

Lena accepted the twenty-cent coins. The older Greeks still

calculated in drachmas. In shops and tavernas the old price was sometimes still visible: drachmas chalked beneath the euro.

She did as she was told and left Alex with Andreas. Unlike most Greeks, Andreas was at a loss when confronted with a child. Sensing this, Alex was quiet. Andreas tapped at the steering wheel. He didn't know how to occupy this boy. He looked around for things to amuse him. Then he remembered the pet shop.

There is a talking bird, said Andreas. Do you want to see?

All right, said Alex, not at all sure what Andreas meant.

Andreas opened the door and the boy climbed out. He walked on ahead, and Alex ran to keep up. This grandfather didn't wait for him or try to hold his hand or anything that adults normally did.

Here! Andreas stopped outside the pet shop. He started talking, urgently, to a flame-coloured parrot. It had green wings and a glossy beak. The bird sat on a metal rail, a chain around one ankle.

He looks sad, said Alex.

No, no. He is a happy bird. He speaks many different languages! Andreas said *Hello* to the bird in English, in French, in German and finally in Greek. The bird made no response. Andreas tried again, this time in Italian.

You're sure it talks?

Always, it talks. Andreas' mood plummeted. It had been a long while since he'd wanted to please someone. He made one last attempt but the bird gave him a defiant look.

It's just a bird, said Alex. It's OK. We can come back another time. This strange old man had been trying to amuse him. Alex was alert to those occasions when grown-ups could not conceal their disappointment. He could sense when they were trying and getting nowhere and he felt sorry for them.

When Lena got back she saw them standing uncomfortably outside the car. Both slightly bow-legged, arms crossed, awkwardly silent. What struck her was the family resemblance. The stance, the arms, the expression.

OK? She looked at Alex.

OK, he replied.

Edáksi? she asked Andreas.

All OK, he said, his voice heavy. You have the tablets? The water?

Yes, she said.

Good.

Back in the car, Andreas said, Even if the wine is good, sometimes it gives headaches. Be careful! They started off again, the car sputtering. Alex hummed in the back seat over the noise of the engine and the tension began to lift.

The road ran up through the mountains past groves of olives and gnarled vines. Here it was fertile land. As they climbed higher the landscape kept changing. Hills of stone rose up at the side of the road, extending into the distance. The stonescape seemed prehistoric, nothing seemed to grow here. Alex was entranced by the hills and the winding roads. The rocks were strange shapes as if they'd been deliberately carved that way.

Alex kept leaning over the front seat, tapping Andreas on the shoulder pointing things out – the face of a horse, a dinosaur, a dog.

Good imagination. Andreas looked approvingly at Lena.

Alex was excited by the old noisy car (in Australia he'd never seen one like this), but most of all by this strange quiet man. This grandfather.

The boy's enthusiasm soothed him and Andreas relaxed. In Apeira, where Marsoula lives, most people came originally from Crete, he said. My parents – *your grandparents* – he turned to Lena, as if it had just occurred to him – they had the Cretan accent. They would say *óshi* instead of *óhi* for *no*. Even Marsoula still says *oshi*.

But you don't have a Cretan accent?

No. Not now. I lost it. Andreas was silent for a time. He dived into some private sadness and Lena felt obliged to haul him out of it.

What time are we seeing Marsoula?

For *mesimerianó*. For lunch. Later. He was deliberately vague. She will wait.

From the back seat, Alex ventured a question: Is she like you?

Marsoula? Andreas paused.

Yes.

Andreas looked at Alex through the centre mirror and then glanced quickly at Lena. We are very different people! Different lives. Her whole life is service to the family. She's a happy person. He looked at Lena and repeated, *We are very different people.*

Lena shifted uneasily in the front seat. Checked Alex's reaction in the rear-view mirror.

Andreas continued as if speaking to himself. Simple people are always happy. They are built for it. Of course, she resents – how could she not resent? I was away. I got an education. I brought shame to the family. One half, anyway. Pah! He laughed. But Marsoula stayed and did her duty.

She never married? Lena asked.

No. There was a man, once, but our father did not approve. But she has her friends here. Everyone loves Marsoula. She has the Church. She is not lonely. A simple life, he said again. Of course she is happy. He addressed Alex this time. The people came from Crete in two waves, he went on, abruptly leaving the topic of Marsoula. It was a topic which pained him. After the War of Independence and then after the German occupation . . .

He likes to lecture, to tell us things, thought Lena. To deflect a difficult emotion he comes out with a fact.

You liked teaching? she asked.

For a time, I enjoyed it very much, he said. You must help the student to question. To challenge. To think. But the education here is all *mathéno apékso.* Learning by the heart. *O papagálos.* The parrot. He checked that Alex had understood the word. The talking bird came to mind and he flushed, remembering his humiliation. *Why hadn't the bird talked?* He braked suddenly and blasted the horn at a black goat which had stumbled into the road. The goat stood in front of the car until he blasted the horn again.

Quite sharply he turned to Lena. Your mother thinks I betrayed her?

Well ... she paused. Not sure how much she should say in front of her son. She looked over her shoulder and caught Alex's eye. Yep. That's about it, said Lena. She was learning to roll with Andreas' sharp turns of thought and conversation.

There are many kinds of betrayal, he said.

I suppose so.

There was a silence. Then he said: In Greece we know this well. Look at our history! The Turks, the British, the Americans. Churchill, Stalin. Pah! But there is a certain kind of betrayer. The informer, the stool pigeon. This is the worst, he said.

Lena wondered what all this had to do with her mother, with personal betrayal, which seemed an entirely different issue. She sensed she was in for a history lesson.

You know this Greek word, for the informer?

No.

O hafiés.

Lena repeated the word.

Hafiés. In the back seat, Alex also repeated the word.

Andreas thumped the wheel. Bravo! Andreas was delighted. He will learn the Greek yet.

*

They parked at the base of a steep slope and Andreas cut the engine. To their right the valley fell away, green and silent. To their left, the village of Apeira was white against the hill. The whole village was built from marble. The walkways and houses all carved into the side of the mountain. *Epitélous*. At last. He pointed up to the village. We are here.

They followed Andreas up along marble paths and through the white arches. He was looking for a kafé. They walked past a waiter sluicing the outside tiles with bleach and water. The waiter smiled and beckoned them through. The kafé was empty with polished wooden floors and huge windows overlooking the valley.

How about this one? Lena said.

Not here, said Andreas. The smell of bleach caught him and he started to cough. He put his hand on her elbow and steered her past. He dropped his arm, turned his face away and coughed again. He had a flash of a room overlooking Attica, himself on the floor. Sometimes this happened. A smell, the sound of a voice, a slant of the light, a time of day. Anything could trip him. How tempting to follow the man on the floor, what happened next. He had to pull himself back. Instinctively, he rolled his shirtsleeves down further.

The bleach? said Lena.

He cleared his throat and didn't say anything.

They walked further down along the marble path, bleach and water running along the gutter behind them. They came to another kafé. It had an open balcony with clear plastic awnings shut against the wind. At the far side of the hill, over the valley she could see a goatherd and his animals scrabbling for a foothold.

This one, said Andreas. Here is good.

They ordered coffees and a hot chocolate for Alex. She took Alex to the bathroom and then came back to the table. While they waited, Andreas rubbed at his arms. He stood up and went to the door and looked up and down the alleyway as if looking for someone, then shut the door and came back again. He seemed agitated. He pulled at the cuffs of his shirt. Lena could see where the scars started at the wrist. She said, All those years ago. What happened to you?

He pulled out his cigarettes and placed his lighter on the table. He seemed about to say something when he saw Alex making his way across the room. He saw the boy pause in front of the pastry display and look over towards them. He heard Alex call his mother over.

Later. He inclined his head towards the boy, clicked his tongue. Your son is wanting you.

*

There were things he could never tell this daughter. Things he could never tell this grandson.

There were times when the night fell in and the house wound tight as a shroud. Times when every detail of every room revealed itself differently. When everywhere he looked there were implements of cutting, blinding, burning: buried in drawers, embedded in walls, hidden in lampshades. As if all the parameters of the room – the floor, the roof, the corners could rise against him at any moment like weapons from long ago. In such moods, the house seemed complicit in his destruction. The walls craved the impact of his body. The bench was there to wound him. How easy it would be, what consolation, to push off from the balcony, like a bird. On such nights, he wanted the obliteration of thought, the erasure of self. There was a strange comfort in physical pain. He knew it after all. He'd survived it. He bore its traces in his bones and on his skin. It seemed that after all these years, despite his best efforts, the tormentor had worked his way inside. The tormentor knew his weak points and his capabilities. Knew how to crush and where to bind. Knew where to press and where to pull. Knew him inside out.

On such nights, if he caught it in time he'd force himself out through the front door. Once outside he'd walk quickly, looking back every so often like a man pursued, trying to put as much distance between himself and the house as possible. He'd run out into the fields or up into the mountains. He would remember to call the dog, which was wary when it sensed these moods. He would stay out in the fields until first light and make his way slowly back, the dog shadowing him.

Other nights when he was not so lucky he'd take to the floor and sit with his back against the wall, head down, pressed against his knees. Unable to move forward or back. Names besieged him. *Irini.* He could see her living a different life, a normal life in another country with a husband and children. Sometimes he saw her with Stavros – he never forgot a name. Some nights, Andreas would see it clearly: a flash of light, the fire in her hands, a man running. But his mind could not stay there. Occasionally he would imagine her at his door, unchanged, her hair about her shoulders and him at her feet, asking for absolution. He would sit there on the floor with this tumult in his head, unable to sleep. Eyes open. Waiting for blows which never came. Waiting for dawn to release him.

He had a routine before bed. A routine which kept the night-terrors in check. Every night for years, before going to sleep, he'd lock the cutlery drawer. He'd put the key under a hessian sack at the far end of the store cupboard. Sometimes he'd put a large stone on top of the sack, just to make sure. Then he'd take everything out of the cupboard and put everything back in. The mops and brooms and buckets. The tins of oil and casks of wine. Every night in a different order. He knew where to find the key and put obstacles in his way. He created a labyrinth for himself. He knew, rationally, that if he could slow himself down and slow his breathing that he would not get at the key to open the drawer of knives. He feared that one night he would forget, that the key would be in the lock, that it would be so easy to pick up a knife and slash at his own reflection. He tried to be careful. In the long years since prison, since the time of the bench and the belt and the fist, since the time of the walls and windows and ragged table edges, he'd managed to be careful. Since his time on the prison island. *O hafiés. Who was the betrayer? Who was the betrayed?* It had become a habit, a reflex action. He'd become used to placing obstacles in the way of the biggest possible danger to his safety, the biggest threat to his life, the tormentor: himself.

*

Behind him Andreas could hear Alex asking for a cake.

We'll be eating soon, Lena said, looking back over at the hunched figure of Andreas. You don't need a cake now.

Andreas brought himself back to the present moment. To the taste of the cigarette on his tongue. To the English words of the boy. To the waiter moving around behind the counter. He tried to earth himself. He turned around and forced himself to smile.

Choose any sweet you want, he said to Alex.

You don't have to, said Lena.

I want to, said Andreas. Lena walked back to the table. Alex gazed at the cakes, so many of them, so many unfamiliar words, and ran back to his mother and put his arms around her neck, aware of the strain on the new grandfather's face. There are too many, said Alex. Andreas tapped out another cigarette. He was about to get up and buy the child something then changed his mind. There was something he needed to tell the girl. He lit the cigarette then turned back to Lena: I never loved your mother.

Lena sat back. A conversation with him was a path full of pot-holes and black ice with a sheer drop either side.

Well. You got her pregnant. She said this in Greek, aware that Alex was all ears.

That is easy, he said. To make a child is easy. He glanced at Alex, hoping the boy wouldn't understand. He, too, switched to Greek. But not for a life together. It was a mistake.

A mistake?

He looked at her hard. As if for the first time he realized

exactly what this mistake had produced. A living grown person:
a daughter.

I liked her very much. She was a beautiful girl. *Ómorfi!* Blonde.
Clever. She was the English teacher of my sister. We met in
Athens. She was a teacher, he repeated, like you.

I'm a dancer, Lena said. I teach dance. Wanting to distance
herself from her mother, that old reflex. She reached for one of
Andreas' cigarettes, fumbled for the lighter in her bag, ignored
her child's disapproving look. So, tell me about you and my
mother, she said.

He tapped out a cigarette for her and threw a memory net
back to the past. What to tell this girl? This daughter. What to
tell her that wouldn't scald and burn and hurt?

I don't remember so well, he said.

You were a *kamáki*, I'm pretty sure of that.

You know about the *kamáki*?

Harpoons, she said. Greek men after foreign women. Of course
I know. She'd had first-hand experience, she wanted to say, in
kafés, on the streets, outside Monastiraki station for God's sake. On
her first trip to Athens she'd been young and learnt quickly.

I *was* a *kamáki*, he said. Not any more.

Thank God for that, she said.

He laughed. For the first time that day.

He'd fallen for a lot of women in his time and they'd fallen right
back. Especially the foreigners. He had vague memories. Most of
them he'd forgotten completely. But he did remember this
woman, this Catherine. She was ten years younger. They'd met in

a kafé in Exarcheia, not far from the Polytechneio. Although he was in love with Irini, it was complicated. But this Catherine was uncomplicated. It seemed so easy with this *xéni*. Nothing serious. He remembered her freckled skin and pale eyes; the pale hair. The way she laughed and moved in her mini-skirts – at ease, confident in her body. It was just before the Colonels.

This daughter, though. He took a draw of his cigarette and looked at her. She was his. Unmistakeable. She was dark, like him. Hair and skin. But she looked wan and tired, black circles under the eyes. She was thin, too thin. She had his eyes. Aegean eyes, the girl's mother used to tell him. He frowned to himself.

What's wrong?

You have my eyes. He paused. So does the boy. Alex's eyes were huge over the rim of his hot chocolate. They bring nothing but trouble.

Only if you go looking, she countered.

He laughed again. He had a sudden urge – who could say where it came from? – to protect her from trouble. This daughter he'd never known or wanted and who'd meant nothing to him. She seemed so slight and small and vulnerable. Like a child, he thought. *His child*. He wanted to say: Tell me of your troubles. But he resisted. He called for more water and the waiter placed a jug down on the table. Andreas filled their glasses. I left your mother because I didn't love her. But it was more than that.

You abandoned her . . .

It's not so simple.

He held up his right hand with the half-smoked cigarette

between the thumb and forefinger. First I will tell you this. He took a long drag on the cigarette. Back then, so long ago! He looked at her with reproach, as if she were forcing him to remember something difficult.

Lipón. He cleared his throat. The Junta take power. The political situation is not good and your mother wants to leave. She wants me to go with her. We are together only a short time. Some months. Her family are worried, they do not want her to stay in Greece and so I tell her the truth: there is someone else and that I cannot go to Australia. Your mother cries, she hits me in the chest, calls me *maláka* and many other things. She returns to Australia. A few months later I am disappeared. She thinks that I have gone with this other woman. It was the *áshimi katástasi*, he says, shaking his head. The bad situation.

For my mother. Lena suddenly had a glimpse of her mother as someone else. A person in her own right: young, mini-skirted, in love. Waiting for someone who didn't love her enough. You want me to feel sorry for you?

No. He seemed surprised. Not at all.

Lena moved her hand and knocked her water glass. Water spread all over the table. The old clumsiness.

So, you left her and then you disappeared? I don't get it.

I went to prison.

Prison?

I was disappeared, along with many others ...

What? This was the first Lena had heard of it.

In 1967 they put me in prison. Then they sent me to the

117

prison island. He hesitated. He did not mention Irini's name and what had happened after.

But the relatives in Athens . . .

He groaned. Lambros and Fotini?

Yes. They said you went to Paris . . .

That was later, he said, annoyed. After the island camp . . .

Did Catherine know? About prison?

He looked at her steadily. Not at first. But later, yes. From Marsoula.

She never said.

Why should she?

And if you hadn't gone to prison?

Ti?

If you hadn't gone to prison and you knew she was pregnant? Lena sounded forlorn, her voice plaintive. Even though she knew the answer she still persisted: Would you have gone to her?

He took a deep inhale. No, he said. Of course not.

*

The words stretched out between them. Lena felt stung. She wanted to ask more but at that moment a small stout woman came into the kafé. Her hair was grey and curly and cropped short. She moved lightly, almost on the balls of her feet. She scanned the tables. She had Andreas' eyes and Lena knew who it was at once.

Andreas called over from the corner, We are here!

Marsoula strode over trying to hide her impatience, Lena

could see it in the set of her mouth, her determined step. *Movement never lies.* She opened her hands wide when she reached the table and couldn't contain herself any longer: I waited for you! She directed herself at Andreas. You did not come! I am waiting. Then I am looking for you . . .

Andreas said in a bored tone, *Kátse*, sit. Now, we are coming. She sat heavily and looked at Lena and then at Alex, appraising them frankly. She smiled. Forgive me. My brother lives for himself, does not think. I am Marsoula, she said in English, extending a hand.

I'm Lena.

The daughter? She looked at Andreas for confirmation, although she knew it was true.

The daughter, he repeated, angling slightly away.

The grandson? she asked happily.

Yes, said Andreas.

Kalosírthate, she said in Greek, and then in English, Welcome! She beamed at them, all annoyance with her brother forgotten. She's good-looking! Marsoula said to Andreas in Greek, thinking Lena wouldn't understand. But so thin!

Nai. Vévea! Of course.

And the boy! Beautiful.

Of course, said Andreas gruffly. There was a brief, still moment in which Marsoula and Andreas regarded each other. Andreas seemed about to say something more. He looked from the boy to Marsoula but she frowned at him and shook her head.

But Andreas couldn't let it rest. You knew about the boy?

Yes, she said, without hesitation. I knew about the boy.

Lena, for her part, appraised the brother and the sister. Aware of something stretched tight between them.

Éla, Marsoula said, avoiding her brother's eye, getting up from the table. *Prépi na fáme.* We must eat!

Lena turned to her son, suddenly aware that she'd ignored him completely for the past half-hour. Alex is hungry, aren't you, Alex? He glared back at her. Already, she was projecting into the future. How she would explain all this to him when he was older. The time they met this grandfather and this auntie. The time on the island. She realized that there were conversations that she needed to have here, whether Alex was present or not. Whether it was difficult or not. She could explain it to him later.

She ruffled her son's hair. I'm sorry, kiddo, she said. We should have some lunch.

You spoke in Greek, Alex said helplessly. All this time. His face was red. What were you saying?

He'd sat quietly until now while the strange words rained down. He felt lost in a flood of words. He'd tried to make sense of the conversation between his mother and this new grandfather, but they'd left him behind long ago. Even the English confused him.

She speaks Greek? Marsoula glanced at Lena.

Nai, said Andreas without enthusiasm. She is full of surprises.

You are hungry, Alex? Marsoula slowly sounded out English words.

Alex nodded.

120

Éla, come! Marsoula took Alex's hand in hers and walked ahead of them out of the kafé. The boy is hungry! She threw the words over her shoulder at Andreas as an accusation. They followed her down marble steps, past an old *foúrnos*. Marsoula was a decade younger than Andreas, around the same age as Lena's own mother, but her dress, her manner, made her seem much older.

Here, is the best biscuits, the best bread on all the island, Marsoula called back to them, pushing Alex in ahead of her, disappearing inside the bakery shop. *Éna leptáki!* she called, then in English, Just a minute!

As they waited outside, Andreas' mood shifted. Lena had an image of Andreas as a man on a tightrope. He could fall at any minute; she sensed that there was no safety net. Her childhood image of her father disappearing into thin air; floating away on a sea of balloons. It no longer seemed so fanciful. Andreas seemed constantly to absent himself and then return from some difficult place.

Everything from Apeira is best! Andreas muttered. Marsoula has all the bad habits of Apeira. *Merde!* They think they are the best on the island. Next time, down in the *Hóra*, you must check. The doctors, lawyers, all have Apeirot names. They think they are the educated ones. All poets and philosophers. Andreas smiled to himself. But Marsoula is not one of them. Marsoula is a simple, traditional woman.

Lena bristled at the superior tone. Nothing wrong with that, she said.

But – he shook a finger at her – I am neither simple nor traditional.

I never said you were.

Marsoula emerged at that moment with paper bags full of biscuits and bread and fresh cake. Alex held one bag and munched on a biscuit, holding it up to show his mother. She could tell from his expression that he was happy. This new auntie gave him plenty of attention. Lena felt relieved.

Marsoula seemed to glide through the marble streets. Everyone waved to her and she had a word for everyone. Lena was instinctively drawn to her.

The house was up winding steps, white and pristine like all the other houses, with a blue door and a brass doorknocker. As her aunt climbed the steps Lena could see the small dimples at the back of her knees where the socks did not quite reach.

Inside, the place was dark and packed in the traditional Greek way. Every surface covered. The walls were full of framed photographs of children and stern elderly women and men in uniform. There were cushions and wall hangings. Dark heavy furniture and chandeliers. Sideboards and dressers covered with lace cloths.

Marsoula motioned them to sit and then went to the fridge and brought out a bag of fish. Fresh! You like the fish?

Lena said that yes, she loved fish.

And the boy?

Alex followed Marsoula into the kitchen, saying that he liked fish fingers. He came running out again when he saw her gutting and skinning the fish.

They have eyes! Alex ran to his mother. Yuck! And then ran back in for another look. Lena laughed. Andreas smiled a tight smile.

They sat in the dining room where the table was already set. Marsoula placed bread in a basket lined with a white napkin next to a small plate of olives. There was a jug of water on the table. She went back and forth with various dishes: *hórta* and rice, *maroúli* salad, stuffed tomatoes. She went down into the basement to get wine. She moved easily between the table, the sink and the stove. She was one of those women who could do several things at once. Such women could rule the world, thought Lena. She was in awe of such women. Dance had taught her to focus intensely – but only on one thing at a time.

Let me help, said Lena, but Marsoula wouldn't hear of it. She sat there watching her aunt through the doorway into the kitchen. Watching her son run to and fro. Lena folded and unfolded her napkin, sipping at her water, unnerved by Andreas' silence. He tapped his fingers on the chair arm.

Eat! Marsoula called out.

We'll wait for you, said Lena.

Éna leptáki. Marsoula finished frying the fish and then brought a huge platter over to the table and finally sat down.

Yeía mas! Lena raised her wine glass.

Yeía mas! they all said. Andreas roused himself and they clinked glasses. He turned to his sister and inclined his head in Lena's direction. Be careful, he said to Marsoula. She is *dinató potíri*.

Hard glass? Lena translated quickly and literally. You mean, she smiled – she thought he was joking – hard drinker?

Nai.

She was shocked when she saw that he meant it.

You mean, for a woman? she said. How much had she had to drink yesterday? She'd smoked more than she'd drunk, that was for certain.

Andreas was playing some odd game. Putting distance between them in front of his sister.

Here in Greece, the women do not drink.

You encouraged me, she said, trying to make light of it. I was being polite. *Kaloksiméroto*, remember? Your own good wine. Where I come from, it's not an issue. She was sounding defensive. She was making it an issue. *Den íme methisméni!* She appealed to Marsoula in Greek and English. I'm no drunk!

She likes to drink. Andreas turned to his sister. She had a headache.

For God's sake! Lena pleaded with him.

Marsoula put a hand on his arm. Andreas – stop! Be kind. And then, in an aside to Lena, He does not know, sometimes, how to be kind. He turns, like so. She held up her hand and turned her wrist anti-clockwise and then back again.

Don't worry, said Lena, looking down at her plate. I'll be careful. And then, making a show of leaving her wine and picking up her water glass, ignoring Andreas, she said, You knew my mother?

I know her well. Still. Every year, a card on my name day.

We knew she had a friend, in Greece . . .

But not the auntie . . .?

No. Nothing. She didn't tell me nothing. Lena used the Greek double negative.

It was for the best. Marsoula reached out and patted Lena's hand. We agreed. Your mother does always for the best. She paused, she couldn't resist: Unlike my brother . . .

Andreas shrugged and reached for the *hórta* and rice. I do as I do, he said.

Marsoula continued, We lived in Athens then. Your mother was my teacher of English. The foreign girls, how they travelled! Incredible . . . Her voice trailed off. I wanted to go to the university. I wanted to travel. To learn the English. These days, I don't speak the English very much. Most of the *xénoi* here are German. She looked over at Andreas. I introduced them – your mother and my brother. Your mother liked him straight away. She glanced at Andreas again. I don't know why. He had many girlfriends, he was a *kamáki* and I warned her, but she didn't listen . . .

And then the whole *katastrofí*.

Listen to him, said Marsoula. Just listen. *You* are the *katastrofí*, brother.

Kríma, said Andreas. Pity.

Andreas got up to go to the bathroom. He's arrogant, said Marsoula, her voice down to a whisper. But he was not always so *páno-káto*. So up-down. Like Andreas, she spoke in a mix of Greek and English. He saw too much. He lived too much. He is not a bad man. Marsoula reached over and held up Lena's wrist ... So thin! Eat. You must eat. And here – she refilled Lena's wine glass and then filled her own. She raised her eyes to heaven. Drink. Do not listen to him.

I'm glad I've met you, Lena said.

Andreas came back into the room at that moment. As he sat down he addressed Lena: But – you are not glad to meet me? He recharged his glass, careful not to look at her.

I'm not sure, Lena said. I'll wait and see.

He remained silent for the rest of the meal then went outside to sit and smoke on the balcony. He took a newspaper with him. He could hear Marsoula questioning the girl, wanting to know about her life in Melbourne. There were so many Greeks there, he heard Lena saying. One day Marsoula must come.

Alex heard children in the street and asked Lena if he could join them.

Lena hesitated. Let him go, said Marsoula.

Alex smiled at his auntie and gave Lena a pleading look. She nodded. OK, then. As he ran out of the house she called: Don't go too far, Alex.

They are safe here, said Marsoula. Nothing can happen.

Alex ran out to play with two young Albanian boys. Lena could hear them racing toy cars down the hill. She sat with Marsoula and told her everything. It all poured out: Johnny's death, her operation, about how she found her mother difficult. Marsoula held her hand and listened. Lena wanted to stay in that room forever. The door to the balcony was slightly ajar. From time to time Lena could hear Andreas scraping the chair or turning a page. After half an hour or so Marsoula brought in coffee and sweets and called him through but he said no, he needed cigarettes. He would go to the *períptero* and be back soon. Then we should go. He looked over at Lena. Soon it will be dark.

Lena called Alex from the balcony to come in and he dragged himself through the door, tired and happy, and promptly fell asleep on the sofa.

You are staying on the island how long? asked Marsoula.

Three days.

Only?

Yes.

But you must stay longer!

They hadn't heard the front door open. Andreas came in, cigarettes in hand, bringing a chill into the room. He'd caught the end of the conversation. If they go, they go, he said.

Ignore him, said Marsoula.

Lena turned away and went over to Alex, trying gently to wake him. She sighed. Her scar hurt as she bent down. He's too heavy for me to carry, she said.

I'll carry him, said Andreas. He moved quickly to the sofa and bent down to cover the boy with his jacket. It's late, he said. Then, scooping the boy to his chest, he made his way to the front door, down the steps and into the cold. The mist was rising up from the valley. *Yeía sou*, he called back to his sister, as if it had just occurred to him to say goodbye.

Marsoula stood in the doorway, a hurt look on her face. She

hugged Lena to her. Stay longer, she said. Come to see me again!

Lena smiled. We'll let you know.

Andreas was quiet on the way back to the car, carrying his grandson, walking ahead. He looked down at the child occasionally and grimaced as if debating with himself. Alex woke up as they neared the car and Andreas put him down, gave him over to his mother. Once they were inside, Andreas took a deep breath, leaned forward with his hands over the steering wheel and said, I'm sorry.

For arguing with Marsoula? For being an arsehole? Lena didn't hold back.

He didn't say anything more. He put the key in the ignition and pressed at the buttons for the radio, trying to get a signal.

I'm sorry you don't get along. I like her a lot.

We are different people.

Families are full of different people, Lena snapped. That's what family is about.

Family is nothing but trouble, he said. He took a quick glance at her.

She understood the sentiment – had felt it plenty of times herself – but she kept quiet.

And now, he said, a child who hates me!

I don't hate you. Her smile was strained. Just – don't tell me what to do. OK? I'm a grown woman. If I want to have a drink, I will. Whether you approve or not. I have my own life. I've lived a whole life without you.

You want your freedom?

Always.

In this we are alike. He seemed to relax then. Before they moved off, he turned to Alex in the back seat, tucked the jacket in tighter around him, saw that he was comfortable. As he put the car in gear he smiled and hummed a little to himself, lost in some private satisfaction. Lena shut her eyes and leant her head against the window. She was tired. She sensed in Andreas nothing that she could hold on to. She realized she would have to be strong, she would have to be different in her dealings with him. She could not be like a small cat, making direct for the person who did not like animals. She would need to shield herself.

Alex slept on in the back seat. Lena watched the villages pass by in the dark car window. Andreas tried to get the radio to work, then gave up.

As they drove into the *Hóra* they could see the Portara lit up from below. They were silent in the car. As they pulled up along the *paralía*, Andreas said, You are here for two days more?

Yes, said Lena. We think so.

I will see you tomorrow?

If you'd like.

And the boy.

If you'd like.

Edáksi, he said. OK.

Kaliníhta, Andreas.

Alex clambered over the front seat. *Kaliníhta*, Andreas!

Until tomorrow, said Andreas.

Alex stood there waving until the car disappeared round the corner. He waved until his small hand hurt, hoping for a sign from Andreas, disappointed. He didn't look, he said to Lena. He didn't see me.

They had a family tradition of waving until the person was out of sight. But with Andreas there were no family traditions. He doesn't know us, Lena said, trying to conceal her own disappointment. She took her son's hand as they climbed the steps into the *Kástro*. We will have to teach him.

6

Early the next evening, they met Andreas in a kafé down near
Agios Giorgos. It was one of the few kafés open at this time of
year and it was smoke-filled and dark, just up from the beach. A
large-screen television dominated the far corner and a table of
men were watching a football game. At another table men played
cards. Lena was the only woman in the place and Alex was the
only child. They sat near a smaller screen showing news from
Athens. Then the door pushed open and a woman with long
black hair came in. She walked through the phalanx of men in a
vest and shorts and long cardigan, tall in her heels.

The prostitute, said Andreas, under his breath.

There's only one?

No. Many. Poor Russians. Poor Chinese. They come to the
island for the better life! Pah! Lena looked around uncomfortably. All the men turned their attention to the woman up at
the bar. The woman ordered a frappé and the men slowly
returned to the television. Andreas often came here to watch the
football or the news, he said. He didn't like television and didn't
have one at home. But he needed the news. He read two
newspapers a day. He would stop and go into a taverna or a kafé

if it was the news on television, he said. He couldn't help himself.

An old habit, he said. I like to know what is happening.

But now it was the football. He gestured towards the screen and nodded a curt hello to a group of men. It was a European game and he hadn't thought that the place would be so full. He'd hoped that Stefanos would drop by as he sometimes did, en route to his own bar, to talk football, to have a coffee, so that Andreas could see his reaction to the daughter and to the grandson. Now his plans were disrupted. The place was too busy, he felt exposed and he was regretting the decision to come.

Three men came over and Lena could feel him tense. Andreas put his head down, hunched his shoulders as if trying to disappear. She wondered what he would say. He hesitated a moment and then introduced them as family, from *Afstralía*.

From *Afstralía*!

Yes, said Andreas. On my mother's side.

She speaks Greek, said Andreas. And this is her son.

The men ruffled Alex's hair. One gave him a wrapped sweet from his pocket.

Bravo! From Melbourni? said one man. My cousin Theo is there. Theo Matsis. You know him?

It's a big place, Lena said, smiling.

Just then, a goal was scored and the men moved off. Andreas was relieved, lifted his head, straightened his shoulders.

She swallowed hard. *Family from Afstralía?*

I must get accustomed. *A daughter. A grandson.* He shrugged.
It will take time.

She stirred some sugar into her coffee and didn't look at him.
It was true, she conceded. *Family from Australia.* He wasn't deny-
ing her outright. After all, she'd used the same line in Athens with
Lambros and Fotini.

They sat there watching the news from the mainland. Lena
sipped her frappé slowly. She saw that Alex was happy with his
orange juice and Andreas ordered a Greek coffee. Suddenly the
news flashed up. More riots in Thessaloniki, in Athens. Police
had beaten a protestor and things had got out of hand. The
barman turned the volume up. Just as suddenly, Andreas was on
his feet, gesturing and yelling at the screen: *Ái sto diáolo!* Lena
translated quickly, Go to the devil. The kafé went quiet and the
men from the football corner got out of their seats. Some came
over to where they were sitting.

There were nods and angry words. *Oi bátsoi.* Cops.

Andreas turned to her. This problem is from the time of the
Colonels. Before, even. Who trusts *oi bátsoi*? No one. And now
this. These bastards – bad training, no education.

He lit a cigarette and pointed to the TV screen. There will be
trouble, Lena. Big trouble. In the time of the Diktatoría, there was a
special squad of police. Anti-terrorist. No one disbanded this squad.
Not the Left or the Right. Under PASOK and old Papandreou it
doubled. So much for the socialists, he said. *Ax!* Here, the police
are used to doing what they like, so they do anything.

A big man at the back of the kafé whose game of cards had

been interrupted walked past their table to the bar. As he went by he muttered, *Tha se páo sti Léro!*

Lena translated for herself. I'll send you to Leros. It must be an idiom, she thought.

Den íne astío, Andreas retorted. It's no joke. Then, under his breath, bitterly, *Maláka.*

He sat there a while longer, looked back at the man who'd insulted him and said, *Éla, páme.* Let's go. If I knew before that he was here, we would not have come.

Lena turned round for a better look. The man was seated now, huge, spilling over his chair, smoking a cigar. He had summoned the dark-haired Russian to sit on his lap.

Who is he?

The ex-mayor, he said dismissively. *Apó vounó.* From the mountains. He had no time for the man.

You know him well?

From the old days, he said. As they were leaving, they paused in front of the television. Police in riot gear and the arc of petrol bombs blazed across the screen. Andreas opened the door and led them into the street, away from the smoke of the kafé and into the breeze coming off the sea.

You can't go to Athens, said Andreas. He felt unexpectedly protective of the girl and her son. You must stay until it is quiet.

It can't be that bad, said Lena.

Believe me. He put a hand on her arm, and then just as quickly removed it. You must stay.

*

134

Lena arranged to stay for another week, while the unrest on the mainland continued. Their days fell into a rhythm. After breakfast, Alex played with the children around the hotel and Lena explored the *Kástro* and the lanes of the old town. They met Andreas in the afternoon or early evening after his work had finished. Andreas delighted in the history of the island and telling them about it. The Catholic cathedral and the long reign of the Venetians; the education of Nikos Kazantzakis by Jesuits; the renovations to the castle; the problem of the shallow harbour and the protests against expansion. He avoided any personal topics. He could speak of changes in the town and in the village but he could not speak further about himself. Nor did he ask Lena anything personal. They orbited around each other, polite and guarded. It seemed to her that Andreas avoided places where he might see people he knew. If he did, he waved quickly and moved on. She decided not to question it. They would soon be gone. A few days after the riots in Athens they wandered along the *paralía* and stopped in the door of a kafé showing the latest news. Let's go in, said Andreas, and then, to Alex: They have ice cream. Andreas pointed up towards the screen. He said darkly, Some tell that the CIA and the Army are behind the riots. Greece is in a mess and they want another coup . . .

And what do you think?

Greeks love conspiracies. This is what I think. The new American president doesn't need this headache.

Andreas, she said, shaking out a cigarette, what did it mean: I'll send you to Leros?

Tha se páo sti Léro? he repeated.

Nai, she said.

It's an expression. From the old days. From the Junta time. Leros was an island camp. A prison. There were many island camps. It was used as a threat. He paused. Also as a joke.

But he wasn't joking, the man the other day?

He wasn't joking.

What happened to people after the Junta?

Some did well.

Like the ex-mayor?

The nephew of a colonel. A big family of the Right.

And people like you?

Like me? He hesitated. After prison in Athens they sent me to Makrónisos. An island camp. After that, I couldn't get the papers, the police would not verify me. I went to Paris and spent the rest of the time in exile. In 1981 I returned to Greece and got my old job back. After some months a new professor came in our department. He'd been the number one *hafiés* in Thessaloniki. But after the Junta, he tells that he is now a Marxist! Andreas pulled a face. *Ax!* And so I left the university.

And you came to the island?

I came to the island.

And what about the other *hafiés*? What happened to them?

The *hafiés* were everywhere, said Andreas. He swept one hand around as if to encompass not just the village or the island but the whole country. From the time of the World War Two. From the time of the Civil War. The files on citizens are *this* thick. He opened his hands wide to demonstrate. During the Junta it was the taxi drivers, the *períptero* owners. Employers. Everyone had information. *Hafiés* in every school. Every university. What does that do to a people, who to trust?

How could someone do it? Lena shook her head. Give information. Sell someone out . . .

He turned on her suddenly, his voice hard. It is not so simple. Not so black and white.

People saving their own skin? At the expense of others? Under torture I could understand . . .

There is no betrayal under torture, Andreas said quickly. Torture is the betrayal.

But . . . Lena sat up. Not everyone was tortured? Surely? People chose to be informers. Some chose to give information.

You don't know nothing, said Andreas, suddenly riven by shame. What could the girl know of such things? Down the long years he had interrogated himself thoroughly. Always the same conclusion: when he had finally given information, it had been his own choice. No one had forced him. No one had held him down. Irini's face came to him and he rubbed at his eyes.

Lena bristled. OK, OK, she said. Keep your hat on.

He touched his head. The hat?

It's an expression.

Argó?

Slang? More like an idiom. *Idiomatikós.*

Idiomatikós? He gave a small laugh and turned around briefly to check on Alex, who had gone very quiet.

Keep the hat on! Andreas said, his mood shifting again.

*

A week after the riots in Athens, they were walking past the ticket office near the harbour. Lena said, I should check the ferry times.

You can check tomorrow, said Andreas. The day after. There is no rush.

I should check anyway, she said. She walked into the ticket office and Alex and Andreas reluctantly followed.

Lena stood looking at the destinations. She wasn't sure what she wanted or where she should go. She was waiting for a sign from Andreas. She'd come to the island to see him and hadn't planned much further than that. She still had plenty of time off work and she could extend it. *Paŕos, Santoríni, Sýros, Mykonós.* They could go anywhere. As the week drew on they'd avoided the topic of leaving. The question was whether she really wanted to go. What more could she learn from this man, her birth father? A man intent on keeping himself hidden.

Andreas sat Alex at a table near the door and then came over to her at the counter. He kept shifting his weight from foot to foot.

Where will you go? he asked. So many places! He looked back at Alex playing with a small replica aeroplane. He was making a runway and a landing strip from brochures. *Soon they would be gone*, he thought. *The boy, the daughter.*

138

I don't know, Lena said. Maybe Santorini. Maybe Crete.

No. No, he muttered.

Sorry?

Lipón. He cleared his throat and looked over at Alex. You could stay. You and the boy. In my house.

With you? She hadn't expected this.

I have room. You can stay. As you wish. You have the holidays?

A few months, said Lena.

Edáksi, he said. It is decided.

Lena stalled a little. She felt a strange desire to stay, but wondered if it would be too much. Andreas was tricky, no two ways about it. He constantly threw her off balance.

I'll have to ask Alex.

Of course.

Then, before she could say anything, Andreas called out: Alex!

The boy looked up and Andreas said in a loud voice: You could stay. In my house. You would like this? You could come to the farm, the *horáfi* . . .

Alex put the toy plane back in its place. He considered his grandfather from a distance. He wanted to run into his grandfather's arms and be lifted high in the air; he wanted this grandfather to be like Johnny. But this grandfather was all sharp angles. He didn't know how to play. There were so many things he would have to teach this grandfather. Instinctively, Alex knew what he had to do.

Yes, Alex called back. Let's go!

He ran over to Andreas and put out his hand. Let's go, said

Alex again, tugging his grandfather to the door, back out into the day.

Andreas accepted the boy's small hand and felt its warmth spread in his own cold palm; felt the warmth spread right through him. How trusting the boy was! How open to life! And he smiled down at Alex and looked back at Lena still standing at the counter. You see. His tone was accusatory. The boy wants to stay!

Lena stood there a minute longer. She was still in two minds. And then it occurred to her: *What would Catherine say?* Of course her mother would be against it. Already she was anticipating the phone call and how she would feel after, leaning against the phone box, winded, as if she'd run a long way to get something and returned empty-handed. Andreas was difficult. *Life was difficult.* She didn't need her mother to tell her that.

*

The next afternoon they moved into Andreas' house in the village. Past the towering agave and the bamboo fringing the road. Up the path that she remembered from the first visit. Andreas insisted on taking her rucksack, pointing out the closed houses of the Athenians and the foreigners as they went.

Here is your room, he said to Lena as they climbed the whitewashed steps up to the house. He pointed to the downstairs room with the shutters open. It has the bathroom, he said proudly. Sometimes though – he made a face – the drains . . .

That's OK, she said.

He showed Alex upstairs to his room. He'd put a small daybed in the study.

Andreas had prepared a meal of chickpeas and rice and they sat out on the top balcony. He tore off some bread and passed it to her. She in turn passed it to Alex.

You don't eat bread?

Not too much.

You don't eat, this is your problem!

Please, she said. *It's my business.* Perhaps this is a big mistake, she thought. Perhaps we should've stayed at the hotel.

Alex looked from his mother to his grandfather. Not knowing what to say, but wanting to please Andreas, he reached for more bread.

Andreas cleared his throat, changed the subject. In the old days – not so long ago – thirty years, maybe – every family had the bread oven. There was no baker on the island. Back then, the roofs are covered in vine branches and sage – like big nests, he said. Wood for the ovens. I like to cook outside. One pot and one fire. *Oréa!* he said. Soon, I will cook for you at the *horáfi.*

Andreas kept talking. Lena understood that he was nervous, and that in his own strained way he was trying to make them welcome.

She relented a little. What about the olive oil? she asked. Do you make it?

He nodded. He then gave them a lecture on olive oil. If the oil is too clear, is no good, he said. He held up his hand to make the point. The oil should be green or gold and *taste* of the olive.

If it tastes acid, the olive is too long on the ground. Macedonians say: never keep oil in a tin. Put it in glass. He paused. A good idea.

Is that what you do? she asked.

No, he said and reached over for more bread. I am not from Macedonia.

She smiled to herself.

A Greek would understand, he said.

And I'm not Greek?

On the island, if you are from Athens you are the *xénos*.

And if you're from Australia? Even if you're half-Greek?

You will always be a *xéni*, he said, matter-of-fact. It's the island way.

*

The first night in the house things did not go well. She'd expected too much. Hoped too much. Wanted everything to be perfect.

She'd opened a door that went off the kitchen. It led unexpectedly to a veranda. She'd startled a tiny bird nesting in one corner. It flew past and into the house, hurling itself against walls and ceilings. Alex began chasing the bird. She yelled at him to stop. Andreas stood still in the middle of the room telling both of them to keep quiet. She was worried that the bird would kill itself and that she would be responsible. Eventually she got Alex to stay put and Andreas approached the bird, now cowering under a stair, its forehead bleeding. He covered it tightly with a dishcloth and went outside. The bird trembled, fluttered under the cloth in his hands, Lena and Alex could see it moving and then it flew off.

Andreas was upset. This bird has lived with me a long time. Every winter, he comes.

I'm sorry, said Lena. I opened the wrong door.

Andreas turned to Alex: The bird was scared. It felt trapped. You should not have chased it . . .

Alex bit his lip and tried not to cry.

It's wounded, said Andreas. The thought of the bird suffering was too much for him. Any creature's suffering was too much.

She shut the door to the veranda. Andreas took his cigarettes from the table and without saying a word, walked out the front door.

Will he come back? Alex started to cry.

He'll come back, said Lena, trying to sound confident.

Around midnight, Andreas returned. He seemed to have recovered himself, Lena thought. He seemed a little drunk.

She said, I'm sorry about the bird, Andreas. I really am . . .

He smiled sadly. A bird is good company.

She hesitated. Does it get lonely here?

No. No. He was emphatic. I have the fields. The donkey. The cockerel. My friends . . .

But, she interrupted, you live alone . . .

I've learnt to live alone. But if loneliness creeps through that door – he pointed to the entrance, to the linen curtain there – I welcome it. I let it in. He had suddenly become expansive; as if performing a version of himself. Someone less inward. Some version of a genial Greek host. Loneliness, my old friend, I ask, What do you want? Something to eat? I make a friend of this loneliness, I sit with him a while. I know his edges. I know the reaches of his voice. When we are done with sitting, I open that door.

Lena watched as Andreas got up and walked to the front door, pushed through the curtain and then came back again, to demonstrate. He pantomimed patting an old friend on the back.

Yeía sou, loneliness, I say. Good night. *Kaliníhta*.

That's brave, she said. It was a good performance. She wanted to clap.

It's the only way. He sat down heavily and she could see him collapse back into himself.

It's late, he said.

She'd put Alex to sleep in the study long ago, dried his tears, tried to reassure him. He'd given up waiting for his grandfather to return.

We didn't know whether you were coming back.

Andreas didn't answer.

She pointed to the pile of dishes at the sink. I'll wash up. I meant to do it earlier.

No, he said. You are the guest. Instead, he handed her a clean bath towel and pointed out an extra blanket for her bed. He stepped back, quite formally, and said, *Kaliníhta*.

Good night, she said.

She went downstairs to her room to get ready for bed. When

she came back up to check on Alex, Andreas had finished washing the dishes. She saw him locking one of the drawers and
opening the store cupboard, a key in his hand. Taking out the
mop and the brush. Taking out the broom and the marble
cleaner. The tins of olive oil. For a moment she thought that he
was going to clean the house. He stopped what he was doing
when he saw her in the doorway. She touched him lightly on the
arm and wished him good night, in Greek this time. He drew
back a little at her touch. She went through to the study to check
on Alex. Then she nodded to Andreas and started downstairs
again. She looked back from the top step to see him deep in the
store cupboard, rearranging its contents.

Once in her own room, she pushed her bags in one corner
and lay down on the bed. All her muscles ached, but her mind
was too full. She worried that she'd be awake all night. She tossed
and turned for an hour and when sleep came it was disrupted by
an image of Andreas running into the distance, then disappearing. There was a dead bird on the ground. Feathers and blood.
He kept looking back like a hunted man. *Why is he running?* her
dream self asked. *What is he running from?*

Athens, August 1967

Stavros Makris is an expert hunter. Birds. Rabbits. Wild boar. *Men. It's all the same to him. He has an instinct for the kill, which is why he has been chosen.*

Íse oti dilónis. You are what you say you are.

These days, he says he is a student, and there is no one to contradict him. He sits in class with his long hair and American jeans and is pleased with himself, pleased with his name although it is not his own. One year before, he'd been a farm boy helping his father in the village. Taking the goods to Kalamata. Hunting in the woods. Fishing in the streams. Then he'd joined the police, been recruited for special duties and sent to Athens. Before April, he'd been an informer involved in Leftist groups. Now he was officially a member of ESA, the military police. Here, at the university, he is whoever he says he is. He will not waste this opportunity. He may even get an education.

He draws himself back to what the professor is saying. He sits there taking notes on the lecture and in the margins, notes on the professor himself. He must remember exactly. He must report back. He does not write in katharevousa — he has no time for the artificial language and cringes when General Papadopoulos attempts it. Privately he agrees with the students around him: the Colonels are ignorant men from the provinces, clowns. He does not want to betray himself as an ignorant man from the provinces. He is no clown.

He disagrees with the students about the 21 April Revolution, although he keeps this to himself. Out loud, at the university, he does not use the word Revolution. He says Junta. *He says* regime. *He whispers* coup *— a word he has recently learnt from his girlfriend, Ioanna, a student of linguistics. Privately he is for the Church, for the family, for* Greece of the Christian Greeks. *He believes that Greece must be purged of all foreign elements. At night he frequents the tavernas and rembetika dives in the backstreets of Piraeus with Ioanna. She tells him she is against the regime. She tells him that* fálanga *is an Ancient Greek word. It means a column of troops, she says. But now it means a form of torture! She looks at him, despairing, helpless, in that way he likes.*

Terrible, he agrees, although he knows it is the best form of persuasion.

He sings loudly to Theodorakis songs in dark smoky rooms — he memorizes lyrics now suspect since the Revolution of April. He sleeps with Ioanna beneath a poster of Melina Mercouri vibrant on one wall.

He enjoys his double life and the benefits it brings. Sometimes he deliberately provokes: Call this a dictatorship? he will say. The tourists see nothing. No hunger, no misery, no guerilla force in the mountains, no shooting in the suburbs. People go to work, make love, go for a vólta in the evenings around Syntagma. He says this in a car full of students en route to a taverna. He is aware of the clandestine duplicating machine in the boot along with the anti-regime posters. They are waved through the occasional roadblock and Stavros gives nothing away.

When he thinks he has pushed things too far he will make a joke. But we have more taxis now, he will force a laugh, more bus stops.

But Papadopolous is no Mussolini, says a thin boy to his left whose father is a German. This is Greece, the boy says. Nothing runs on time. The students make clever jokes about Mussolini and Europe and Fascism and history and Stavros has no idea what they are talking about. He chafes at the ease and knowledge of these young city people. He has to think fast, think on his feet.

He is accustomed to telephone conversations in code: Let's go for coffee *is* always something else. *He believes that he has cracked all their codes.*

He is alert to all expression of anti-national views. Just that morning, a student mocked two soldiers in the street: Greek Army, Greek killers, *the boy said, in English, under his breath. Stavros had quickly translated* Ellinikós stratós, Ellinikés skotóstres, *pleased that he could do this, that he knew these English words. He'd even linked arms with the boy in solidarity. Very clever, he said. He recognized the boy from the history class. He had once heard this boy complain about his grades from the professor. He got the name of the boy and later wrote it down. It would be useful.*

To the Island

Since April any assembly of more than five people needs special permission. Any citizen can be arrested without a warrant. But Stavros enjoys a free pass to all gatherings. Sometimes he believes himself to be invisible and invincible. He is clear as water, he is light as air, he can be in many different places at once. He has many different faces.

But this professor is a problem. With his long hair and his dangerous views; a threat to national security.

He brings himself back to the lecture: 'The Church and the Ottoman Empire'. He yawns, but then something in the tone of the professor makes him sit up, take notice. He detects, or thinks he detects, an undercurrent. He looks around the room. Everyone is sitting to attention, as if a volt of electricity has circuited the hall. His own village does not even have electricity and it is still a miracle to him. He wonders if the professor is speaking in code. He listens carefully now. He hears the professor dispute the established version that the Church, and only the Church, kept the language alive under the Turk. This is not the full story, says the professor. There were other forms of resistance. The facts show that the Church, too, was compromised, grew fat, in fact, under the Turk – some elements even colluded. The professor pauses, rather too theatrically, thinks Stavros, and gestures around the room. In times of tyranny, there is always collusion, he says.

For a brief and terrible minute Stavros believes that the professor's words are for him. That his real identity is apparent. A farm boy from the village, apó horió. He feels his face go hot.

Then he remembers that there are at least ten other informers and ESA men – military police – in this hall alone. He rolls his shoulders, moves his neck from side to side, tries to relax.

The professor's words are so inflammatory, the words fall in such a way that it feels as if the whole hall is holding its breath. Now, Stavros is certain that the professor's words have a double meaning: There are as many ways to collude as to resist. *He hears the words break over the heads of the students. He may as well hand them a bomb, thinks Stavros.* Start with the small ways – *the professor smiles* – start with the language. *He has conducted the whole lecture in the* dimotikí. *He does not use the language decreed by the Colonels. He does not use the language of the rewritten textbooks – but the language of the home and of the streets. He has ignored the rewritten textbook altogether. Stavros notes all this down.*

The night before, Stavros had seen Irini, the professor's girl-friend, in a rembetika place near Monastiraki. She'd come in with a group of students. No sign of the professor. Stavros had not seen them together since April. Stavros had enjoyed himself, his fist high in the air, singing along. He'd been there with Ioanna. He'd recognized some of the other men from ESA – with their long hair and revolutionary ways they could be students.

But they are not students.

Yeía sou, Irini, he'd said to the girl. He'd slept with her once or twice. Before and after the Revolution of April. An attempt to get information. But Irini was so self-contained – secretive, almost – she'd given nothing away about the professor. He'd wondered at the time if she was hiding something. Whether she, too, was really worth following? Then he remembered her family name and connections and dismissed the idea. Her uncle, after all, was a minister in the Revolutionary government.

She'd said hello and then turned back to her friends. He thought she looked thinner, strained. She had not introduced them. It was as if they had never met.

He'd smarted at her tone, her dismissal of him. No matter, he thought, coming back to the lecture and looking at his notes. He has more than enough information and it comes from many sources – the períptero *owner, disgruntled students, an ambitious colleague. Taxi drivers, ticket collectors. Many of these people are not even political, thinks Stavros. Their motivations are greed and self-interest. He smiles to himself.*

Tomorrow, the boy who'd mocked the soldiers will make a complaint against the professor, one of several. The charges against the boy for anti-government activity will be dropped. The file on the professor keeps growing.

Stavros is closing in. He is no longer a man from the provinces, the only one to finish high school from a village without electricity, but a man with a state job, a pension, a sure place in the world.

Stavros Makris, real name Stavros Makropoulos, shifts uneasily in his seat, repeating English words to himself, dreaming of his career in ESA, waiting for the lecture to be over. He wants to work at Bouboulinas Street. He wants to get his hands dirty. Their methods are Greek – fálanga *is an Ancient Greek* word – *but their nicknames are all American. He imagines himself on a Harley Davidson, a blonde at his side. He is wearing sunglasses and his nickname is* Sheriff. *He curses in English as his boot finds its target. Bright colours. Open spaces. The Sheriff in pursuit; guns, fists and blood. No one escapes and the ending is always the same. Stavros puts down his pen and sits back, pleased with himself.*

The Sheriff always gets his man.

7

Kaliméra! Lena could hear a man's voice and a knock at the door. It was morning. The shutters were closed and the room was dark. She had no idea what time it was. Her dreams had been full of her father running on ahead and searching for something or running from someone. Blood on the ground. She woke now, exhausted, as if she too had run a long way into a dark place.

She sat up. Momentarily unsure of where she was. Then it came to her, she was in her father's house – her *birth* father's house – in Greece, surrounded by fields. Andreas was calling her.

Kaliméra, she answered. *Ti óra íne?*

Eftá, Andreas said. Seven o'clock.

She groaned. So early?

She got out of bed and opened the door, leaning against the doorjamb.

Let me show you how to make coffee, he said. He seemed to be in very good spirits. He seemed to have recovered from the night before. She still felt bad about the injured bird.

She said, a little too abruptly, I know how to make coffee.

But the *Greek* coffee, he said in a low voice. How much sugar, how long to boil . . .

OK. But no lectures. It's too early!

OK. This daughter was sharp. He recognized himself in her. But my coffee is best. I am known for my coffee.

Éna leptáki, she said. I need to wash. I need to wake up . . .

I will wait, he said, and walked back up the steps.

When she came up to the kitchen, he looked at her fresh face and damp hair. He thought again that there was something child-like about her. With a pang, he wondered what she'd looked like as a small girl. He said quietly, sadly, turning away, *Ómorfi*. Pretty. The pretty daughter . . .

Thanks, she said. A pretty old daughter . . .

He smiled. You are not so old. But now – the coffee!

He put sugar in the *bríki*, the small saucepan of water, and set it on the gas flame. *Métrio?* he asked.

Yes, she said. She liked her coffee a little sweet. He waited until it boiled and then put in a spoonful of coffee for each cup.

Then you must take it from the flame three times, he said. He urged her over and she peered into the water. Now is best, he said, watching everything swirl and dissolve with an expert eye. Sit.

The daylight was pale and golden. Overnight it had rained. Maybe it will be a good year, he thought to himself. Maybe. The sun was rising as they drank their coffee.

When he had finished, he said, Now I must go to the field.

We'll come with you, she said.

To the *horáfi*? Today? It occurred to Andreas that in a very short time, his life had changed fundamentally. It occurred to him that someone might see this daughter and grandson in the fields and that he would have to answer questions. He'd managed to keep his answers very general so far. Of course everyone was curious about the relatives from *Afstralía*.

Why not? Lena asked.

Just then Alex emerged from the back room.

Would you like to come to the *horáfi*? Lena asked.

Horáfi? He had forgotten this word.

The farm.

Yes! said Alex. Lena marvelled at how quickly children could shake off sleep and leap right into the moment.

You don't have to come, Andreas said, uneasy.

But it's all new for us.

His shoulders slumped a little. She sensed the dip in his mood as they followed him down the track and across the road through fields of vines and gnarled olive trees. Past goats and newborn lambs destined for slaughter at Easter. They stopped to look. One of the goats came up to the fence and nuzzled Alex's palm. Lena and Alex were city people in thrall to the natural world and Andreas watched them, amused.

Andreas called out to the sheep and the goats. He greeted his donkey. He inspected the work from yesterday – was it only yesterday that the daughter and the boy had come to stay with him? He walked quickly. Lena had to hurry to keep up, trailing Alex behind her. Andreas had a small knife and collected herbs as he went. Pushing apart weeds and daisies and the first wildflowers. He held up a bunch of long stringy plants – good for the *nefrá*, the kidneys, he said and patted his lower back – to make the tea.

It took about an hour. He fed the animals, tamped the earth. Pointed out the small green shoots on the vines. *Smell this.* She wasn't good at identifying scents. *Wild sage*, he said. He showed them the herbs pushing up through the limestone, thriving in the dry land. Rosemary and myrtle, juniper, thyme and fennel. He named them in Greek first and she tried to translate into English. All are more strong in the wild, he said. He instructed them as he went, bending down, lifting up, holding out for them to enjoy. Crushing them in his palm, urging Alex to do the same and to breathe in the scent.

He waved to a neighbour in the field opposite but was glad that they didn't stop to talk. He could explain to the neighbours later. He felt relieved. Maybe it would be all right after all. He smiled a big smile.

It's all good. *Kalá*.

He lit a cigarette and leant on the rusty fence and exhaled with satisfaction. He offered one to Lena and they stood there in the early morning with the sound of the donkey and the cockerel, the earth still damp. She stood there with the unlit cigarette in her hand and her son giving her the evil eye. She would light up later. Andreas gave his grandson the bundle of herbs and they made their way back up to the house.

*

The next morning, after coffee, Andreas offered to take them into town. We can do the shopping, he said. As he was loading the car, a small old woman in a headscarf struggled up from the house opposite.

Get in, he said to Lena and Alex.

Quick, he urged.

The old woman walked slowly over to them, bent double with osteoporosis, tapping the ground with her stick.

Kaliméra, Andreas!

Kaliméra, Kiria Sofia!

Kiria Sofia came up to the car and peered in the window at Lena and her son.

Yeía sas, she said to them and looked at Andreas, waiting for an explanation.

They are family, he said quickly. From *Afstralía*.

Afstralía?

Yes.

Kiria Sofia turned back to the car and scrutinized Lena's face. *Yeía sas*, she said. Then, to Andreas, She looks like family. She smiled at Lena, who smiled back. And the boy!

Yes, Andreas said. Lena could see he was uncomfortable, eager to be gone.

Kiria Sofia, we must go now.

Andreas got in the car, started the engine, and moved off. He left his neighbour standing there in the winter light, wrapping her shawl about her and squinting after them, wondering what she would tell Giorgos, her son.

Lena looked out of the car window, trying to make sense of it. Why *should* he introduce her as his daughter? They took the back route down to the *Hóra*, winding down to the harbour. To her right she could see the Portara. Now it didn't seem beautiful. It looked to her like an old door on a bleak empty hill.

How long will you keep this up? she asked. Keeping us a secret.

It's for the best. Andreas dropped his voice as if they had an audience. He sighed. Soon, the whole village will know.

She pushed down her complicated feelings and realized that she was hungry.

You never have breakfast? she asked him.

Óxi! He clicked his tongue, relieved that she wasn't going to argue. Coffee only. Water. A cigarette. What Greek has breakfast?

Well, Alex needs breakfast. And I'm a little hungry . . .

Good, he said. You need to eat.

She sighed but didn't say anything.

They stopped at a bakery near the port. She bought a spanakopita for herself and a fruit bread for Alex.

You have been to the Portara?

Yes. At sunset. When we first got here.

He looked disappointed. We could go now.

She bit into her spanakopita. It was oily and overcooked. *He probably wants to tell us some history,* she thought. She decided to humour him. OK, she said. If you want, let's go. She took another bite and then wiped at her face with a tissue. She was covered in crumbs. She left the rest of the spinach pie uneaten.

You should finish, Andreas said.

Later, said Lena.

Andreas clicked his tongue. He wanted her to eat more, but decided to keep quiet. It was empty up on the promontory and there was a cool wind although the winter sun was gaining strength.

It's on a special line, said Andreas. From here direct to Delos and to other sacred places. To Delphi, even. The Ancients knew this, he said. Also here, Ariadne is abandoned by Theseus.

And rescued by Dionysus, she said.

You know this myth?

I know this myth.

Theseus didn't kill the Minotaur, she mused out loud. He confronted it, she said. Inside himself.

Inside? She could see Andreas working this over.

Inside, she said. We make our own labyrinths. We make our own monsters.

He looked over at her and wondered what she could know of such things. The Greeks had suffered – occupations, forced migrations, the Civil War, dictatorships – and that was only the twentieth century. Now there were hard times coming. Uncertainty. What could a young Australian woman (he thought of her as young) possibly know of such things? Growing up in Australia, what could she know of misery and pain?

They got out of the truck and climbed up to the Portara. Alex walked along behind them. There were no other tourists. They stood in silence for a while looking out towards Paros, framed by the huge marble doorway. *Labyrinths and monsters*. It was bothering Andreas. He cleared his throat. What do you know of suffering?

It came out as a challenge and Lena recoiled. I know a little, she said, defensively. I know enough.

Yia parádigma? He was pushing her.

For example? She turned on him, angry now: I can never have another child. She paused to gauge his reaction. Is that enough for you?

He flinched a little.

Yes, she said and her voice broke. Is this a test?

No. No. He shook his head. But of course it was. He was always testing people. He could see that his question had hurt her and he didn't know what to say, how to comfort her.

But you have a fine boy, he said, awkward now, looking around for his grandson. Alex! he called, trying to distract himself. There was no answer.

Alex! she called.

They'd lost sight of the boy. Lena called again but there was no reply.

He won't be far, said Andreas, hearing the catch in her voice.

She called again. Alex was a child so curious about the world and so dreamy that she often lost sight of him. He'd stop to gaze at an old shoe or a rock. He moved more slowly and mindfully through the world than she did. Andreas put his hand out, trying to reassure her. It is OK, he said. I'll go. He walked calmly back down the path. Though he was feeling far from calm. The *xenói*

160

and their children. So anxious! What could possibly happen to the boy? But when he saw Alex, he stopped short. The boy had climbed down near the cove at the base of the Portara. He was jumping from rock to rock with a great bunch of kelp in his hand. The rocks were slippery and the waves were rough. He could easily fall. Andreas was surprised to feel slightly alarmed himself. If the child fell, he would not get there in time. The boy would be pulled under. But a child had to learn risk, he told himself. They had to learn danger. You couldn't protect them forever.

Andreas called up to Lena. I've found him.

He made his way down carefully and crouched next to Alex on the wet rocks, examined the stones and the bands of kelp he'd collected and drew his attention to a tiny purple iris.

I'm coming, she called to Andreas.

She was out of breath, angry with herself for losing sight of Alex. She'd tried not to run.

Alex! Don't move without telling me. With difficulty, she kept her voice under control.

But I was here!

We couldn't see you.

You were talking, he said. He shrugged and moved closer to Andreas, who was still examining the iris. The boy is fine, he said, without looking up. Leave him. Look! he said.

She wasn't in the mood now to look at a flower.

Soon the wildflowers are here, said Andreas. And then it came to him: Stay until spring, he said, trying to make amends, unable to look at her.

I don't know about that.

Think on it, he said. His knees clicked as he stood up. He brushed the dirt from his trousers and walked on ahead to the car. His hand trembled a little as he opened the door.

*

Towards the end of February the storms started and they woke one morning to find that the back room was leaking. The bathroom was leaking. Several tiles had broken off the roof in the strong winds. They had no power.

We must check with Kiria Maria, Andreas said. She has the telephone. She can ring for us. Go and ask if they have *révma* ...

Révma?

Power.

But I haven't met her. Lena felt shy all of a sudden. I don't think I've even seen her ...

They've been away, he said. In Salonika, visiting their children. They are back now. Yesterday I saw the car – the house on the corner.

Who will I say I am?

Kiria Maria knows, he said, resigned. By now, they all know.

Lena went across the street. Kiria Maria welcomed her in, phoned the electricity company – it was a fault outside, they said – and invited them to *mesimerianó*.

We have to wait for the engineer, Lena reported back to Andreas. And, she hesitated, Kiria Maria invited us to lunch. All of us.

Lunch? The thought of a meal with this new family and his neighbours made Andreas nervous. I'm not sure.

Well, Lena said, matter-of-fact. We have no power. It's cold. We'll have to go somewhere.

You stay, he said. I must go to the town. To get wood. To get tiles. To gather myself, he thought. He wondered if he could avoid this lunch.

When he got back two hours later, in addition to the planks and the nails and containers from the hardware store he had two large boxes of sweets. He had made his decision. He could not refuse the hospitality of Kiria Maria.

Take these, he said to Lena. He called for Alex and led them in a procession across the street. At the door, he took the boxes from Lena and presented the sweets to Kiria Maria, who put a hand up to his face. Like a son! she said. He is good to us. She turned to Lena. He often cooks for us. You should know this. She looked inside the boxes. Exclaimed over the custard pie.

Bougátsa!

Of course, bougátsa, said Andreas. Your favourite.

So good to us, she repeated.

Andreas shook his head, as if to shake off the compliment.

Then she turned her attention to Alex. Ómorfos! she said. Beautiful! Making a fuss of him, handing him a cushion so that he could sit up high and comfortable at the table, Kiria Maria served them chicken soup with rice and fresh bread. She put the boiled chicken on a plate. Lena sat in the warm small house that

163

Kiria Maria had grown up in. They drank home-made wine that her husband Giannis had made. Lena was careful not to drink more than two glasses. Careful not to look at Andreas. She forced herself to eat more than she normally would. All afternoon they sat there, waiting for the engineer to arrive, waiting for things to be fixed. Andreas was quiet. Alex bedded down beside the stove and grew sleepy.

Kirios Giannis came in. Tall and handsome with his white hair and moustache. Andreas stood up and they clasped hands and then Andreas pointed to a photograph of a young Giannis in Syntagma Square. In the photo he had dark hair and was dressed in the white costume, long socks and black shoes of the Evzone, the Presidential Guard.

I was young then, laughed Giannis.

After the introductions he said to Lena: Soon, it will be Easter. You will stay?

I don't know, said Lena. She looked over at Andreas, who shrugged and looked down at the table.

Andreas reached over for more bread. They have no plans, he said.

It is the big time of year. The best time, said Giannis.

Andreas kept quiet. His neighbours knew that he rarely went to the church. They did not know that he found Easter difficult. Easter Friday in particular. He couldn't bear the sound of the cockerel. He couldn't bear to watch the procession of the *Epitáfios* – the coffin of the Christ through the streets – the whole tragic movement of the Easter weekend; the way it played out.

He fixated on the sufferings of the cross. The nails through hands and feet. It plunged him into sadness and difficulty. It plunged him into his own private mourning: *And then she was gone.* He found little comfort in the resurrection.

Andreas reached for the water jug, avoiding the eyes of this daughter. He'd been avoiding the question of when she would leave, taking the boy with her. He was preparing himself for it. Every day he expected an announcement and every day their presence cut deeper into him. Every day the child left his mark; drew him in closer.

Of course they must stay, he said finally, reaching over for more wine. Of course.

*

The days passed and they were developing their own routines. Andreas insisted on cooking for them, he liked to cook, he said. In any case, she must rest, he said. Heal up. She tried to clean the house and keep the place tidy – not easy with a small child. She would go shopping for cheese and bread and fish down in the *Hóra*. She would put flowers in glass jars around the house. Light small candles on the balcony in the evening. She liked to make coffee for Andreas when he came in from the fields – Greek coffee – the way he had taught her.

They had been on the island for a month. Andreas would send Alex down to the well with the canisters for fresh water. He'd struggle back up the hill but he loved this daily task and Giorgos across the street would look out for him, would chat to him in

Greek. Playing with the other children and talking with the adults, just being here, he'd picked up a lot.

Here in the village, Lena felt enveloped in a communal embrace. Only her birth father did not draw her in close. Usually Andreas was away in the fields by the time they woke up. After the first week, he had let her sleep. Most days she hardly saw him at all until late afternoon, when they would have a meal together. Then he would disappear early evening. Into the *Hóra* to see Stefanos, or to watch the news in a kafé or to be by himself. She wasn't sure, as the weeks slid by, whether he even liked having them there. He was sometimes brusque with her. He was wound so tight. As if coiled around secrets and hurts and history she would never comprehend and he would never share. Only occasionally would she sense him uncoil and relax. Only Alex got through to him. He would pull at his shirt. He would bring stones for inspection. The child pushed through Andreas' line of defence; the child as Trojan horse. The child bearing gifts of a flower, a shell, a drachma coin found near the sea. Lena was never sure how to please this birth father. Sometimes she gave up trying. But Alex never stopped trying and to her amazement, he succeeded.

*

Here on the island, sunset was a big event. On clear days Lena would sit watching from the corner of the top balcony as the sun fired down and the birds disturbed the branches; as the cats started to prowl and the sun sank behind the clouds. Some days there'd be huge clouds, the shape of continents. The sun would flare orange then disappear and re-emerge as if through a trap-door, leaving the sky pink and the outline of the smaller islands etched dark against it; a bright disc powering into the sea. Sometimes Andreas joined them on the balcony, sometimes not. Occasionally he would talk to her about the past. She often sensed that he wanted to unburden himself but fear stopped him. *Fear of what?* she wondered.

One evening as they were settled on the balcony, the radio on in the background, Andreas quietly reading the newspaper, everything peaceful, he suddenly leant over, jabbed a finger at the newspaper and said to Lena, Look! He handed her the page. It was a photograph of a hooded Iraqi prisoner, attached to wires, standing on a box. A photo that had been reproduced many times. Yes, said Lena. Terrible. I've seen it before.

It's a crime, he said. The Americans. The British. What they have done there.

Yes, Lena agreed. It's shocking.

We become accustomed, he said. This is the problem. He looked out towards Paros, to the line of the sea to steady himself. He'd seen the photograph many times. Each time it disturbed him.

We taught them well, he said.

She looked up from her own book. What do you mean?

The first cases of torture – documented – are from Ancient Greece, he said. Democracy and torture. He gave a short laugh. Our gifts to the world.

He looked out over the village, rubbed at his arms. Lena wondered what he would tell her next.

In Greece, from the Civil War on, Andreas said slowly, two out of three political prisoners are tortured.

She put down her book, took a punt. And you?

He sighed. Me? He looked down at the tabletop, pulled at the cuffs of his shirt. It was only a short time.

Meaning?

That's enough, he said.

But what did they want from you, she pushed, feeling something withheld, something just below the surface of speech.

He hesitated, annoyed that she was forcing him to speak. Alarmed that he had started the conversation. He shrugged: Names. People against the Junta. He relaxed his arms enough to reach for his lighter. He clicked it open and lit a cigarette, inhaling deeply. He looked drawn, as if the words had aged him. Lena wanted to reach out a hand in comfort but his arms were locked tight over his chest. He shut his eyes and withdrew into himself.

Then, looking around, he said, Where's the boy?

Downstairs, said Lena. He's playing in the street. Alex had started playing with children in the village. She could hear them now, calling to each other in a mix of Greek and English. She could hear them kicking a soccer ball. Dimitris laughing because Alex only knew Australian rules and wasn't used to a round ball.

Andreas opened his eyes and gestured towards the jasmine, wildly scented, wanting to change the subject.

Ákoú ti mirodiá Listen to the smell, Andreas said. Listen!

Winter was easing into spring. Melbourne had a real spring, not like places up North. Not like the West. Yet it was nothing like this, she thought. Andreas was teaching her to pay attention; she was becoming alert to the changes around her. She looked at him sitting there with the paper spread open on the table. *Listen to the jasmine*, he said, turning the page, trying to put all dark things behind him. *My favourite.*

Another evening, Andreas joined her on the balcony. I am here to work, he cautioned. Not to sit! He had shears in his hand and heavy gloves. He had cotton strips to wind around the rubber tree where he cut, to staunch the flow of sap. He extended the ladder up from the balcony and expertly pruned the tree, commenting on the plants next door. He directed her attention to the hibiscus. It bloomed nearly all year, Andreas said. Look! It delighted him. If you cut the hibiscus and put it in water it opens and shuts as if still in the earth, he said. The birds were now noisy, the insects were starting to hum. Everything searching for light and warmth.

You know a lot, she said, about all of this. Plants and animals. She gestured out to the fields.

Ah, but at first I knew nothing. Andreas climbed down from the ladder. He put the shears aside, covered in milky sap. I was a boy from Athina. A city boy. We came back every summer here, to the house of my grandparents. There was the beach. The girls. I knew nothing of the land or the *horáfi*. I didn't want the hard peasant life. I had to learn everything.

How old were you then?

In 1981 – he paused – I was ... She could see him counting back. I was ... forty-five.

Forty-five when you came here?

Nai.

In 1981, I was fourteen.

Fourteen? She listened for any note of regret at what he'd missed – her own childhood – but he continued with his story: I had to learn everything. That the end of September is for the grapes, then the almonds follow. In late winter, the olives are ready. In February I cut the vines. By June I must pick the *hamomíli*, the oregano, the mountain tea. I must let it dry. In autumn, I must sort it. I learnt that the best time for *hórta* is until May. By the end of summer it will taste bitter. I learned, *síga, síga,* slowly, slowly, what to pick and what to leave. The villagers taught me that this life of the land is all waiting, watching. Hoping for rain.

I know nothing about the land, she said. I grew up in the suburbs ...

Ta proástia?

Suburbs, yes. Of Melbourne.

Third biggest Greek *póli*, he said. In all the world. He sat down, despite himself, and lit a cigarette. He looked around for the boy. When he was alone with this daughter he felt anxious or sad. Often he didn't know what he was feeling.

Yes. Many Greeks. You could maybe visit, she said tentatively, one day.

No, he said, with a wave of his hand, dismissing the idea. I'm too old for cities.

OK, she said, smarting at his tone. OK. She looked out over the fields, changed tack. I know nothing of farm life. I'm scared of animals. But I would like to learn . . .

Everyone should learn. In the past, everyone knew. You are scared of the donkey and the cockerel?

She laughed. I don't know.

Alex came upstairs at that moment. Can I go to Dimitri's? Here on the island he was getting used to staying up late, along with all the other children.

Lena looked at Andreas. It's getting late, she said, knowing that he would contradict her. He thought that the English bedtime was a terrible notion – restrictive – he'd told her more than once. What Greek sends the child to bed early?

It's not late, said Andreas, rolling his eyes. Then, to Alex: You like the donkey and the cockerel?

What's cockerel?

A morning bird. *Ki-kiríkou, ki-kiríkou.*

Ki-kiríkou? Alex had never heard such a sound.

Cock-a-doodle-do, said Lena. *Cock-a-doodle-do.*

Andreas gave Lena a severe look. In Greece, we say *Ki-kiríkou.*

Fine, said Lena. It was her turn to roll her eyes. We'll go with the Greek cockerel.

Alex looked from his mother to his grandfather, confused. Is it a bird? he said.

Of course, a bird! said Andreas.

As if on cue, a donkey brayed. A long melancholy sound.

Gaidoúri mou, he said. My donkey. Wait and listen. Andreas turned his head in the direction of the sound, held his palm up. Soon they heard the cockerel in the distance.

You hear? The donkey and the cockerel are old friends. He became animated. They have no sense of time. The old donkey calls out, any time of night or day. When he is lonely he calls out to his friend the cockerel. The cockerel always answers. I am here. Andreas made the sound of the cockerel in Greek again: *Ki-kiríkou. Ki-kiríkou.* When they call to each other, said Andreas, they know they are not alone.

*

With spring coming, and the warmer days, Lena could feel the energy rising in herself. She was trying to get back into her body again. As if she were a spirit who'd slipped her skin. It was over three months since the operation. Andreas got bicycles for them. It was a challenge – cycling and walking everywhere. With the wind and rain at first, then sand storms from Libya spreading red dust. *So much weather.* After she'd acclimatized, she tried to get back to exercise and using the muscles again. She was still fatigued and tender around the abdomen. Standing side-on in the mirror she looked swollen around the scar. She'd never had a belly before and it disturbed her; made her reach for the cigarettes, thrown back on her younger self. *Lose a few pounds*, her teachers would say. She was back there now with the hieroglyphics on her hand – a list of what she'd eaten and how much. Calories consumed and expended. Years of her life devoted to it. She kept tracking down that route and then stopped, put down the cigarettes, took a deep breath. Took hold of herself.

Soon, she said to herself. Be patient. Soon you'll be strong again.

When she was young she'd never really understood the rhythm of days and seasons. Of course there were days when her muscles ached and she'd ease off a little, soak her feet, apply plasters, elevate her legs. But she was oblivious to the day in itself. She'd always had energy to burn. As a kid she used to jump the sprinklers in the back yard. She'd practise her handstands in the kitchen and fall awkwardly against cupboards and chairs. She'd be covered in cuts and bruises and mercurochrome. Johnny had nicknamed her *Tangles*, because she was always falling over. He'd say, You go at everything like a bull at a gate! Even after she became a dancer, became more measured, she still went at everything full-tilt. The operation had changed all that. She'd been unprepared for the shifts and slough of days; every day was no longer the same. On the island this seemed more the case than in a city. The days had completely different rhythms. Sunrise. Sunset. Religious festivals. She no longer knew what to expect of a day or of herself. She watched this father of hers closely for signs; for how a day might unfold.

She kept on, she told herself. She was still here. She performed the simple act of putting one foot in front of the other. There were days when sadness fell – a baby in a pram, a nursing mother, a small boy running past – days that she couldn't anticipate or prepare for. On these days, Andreas was more careful with her. He never again challenged her about suffering, about her knowledge of misery or pain.

All change is good because it takes away the fear of change. She'd read that once and not understood. Here on the island she was closer to some sense of it. On good days, as the weeks went on, she could cycle with Alex down to the beach even though the water was cold. They'd take their shoes and socks off, lean back in the sand dunes, enjoying the low sun. She'd read, sheltered from the wind. He would collect sticks and shells and run around and come back to show her his treasures. He would put them carefully away in the rucksack to show Andreas later. On the beach, they were the only people there.

Of course! What Greek goes to the sea before May? Andreas sniffed. We do not swim before June.

Just to stretch out a toe into the sand, how good it felt. The simplest of stretches. As a kid she used to imitate the stretch of cats and dogs and birds. Spreading her feathers wide or making a nest of her limbs. When she was sad she'd fold into origami shapes in front of the mirror on the wardrobe door. For now, it felt good to stretch her arm to throw a ball to Alex. To extend a foot into the freezing sea. *Start with the small things,* she thought. Start there.

*

In the middle of March they went down to the *horáfi* one afternoon. Andreas wanted to cook for them on the fire outside.

They'd made several trips to the fields with him but this would be different.

We'll have a picnic, Lena said to Alex.

With *Pappoús*?

It was the first time that Alex had used the Greek word for grandfather. In English, at least when she was present, he always called Andreas by name.

Where did you learn that? she asked.

Andreas taught me, he said. *Pappoús* taught me.

Bravo, she said, feeling a stab of something. Somehow Alex had established a relationship with her birth father that went way beyond her. She could never imagine calling Andreas *Babás* or him claiming her as his daughter – *i kóri mou* – in public.

It was a fine day. Red poppies, sparse in February, were now everywhere reaching up through the stones. The rock roses pulsated gold and lavender. The daisies and the chamomile edged yellow along the road. She could see an old couple lifting rocks at the edge of the field.

What are they doing? she asked Andreas.

Looking for snails, he said.

Andreas had built the fire from vine twigs in a pit ringed with large stones. She watched as he chopped potatoes, onions and okra on a stone slab. The tomatoes were already in the pot. He handed Alex a small knife and showed him how to use it.

It's my best thing, he said, to cook outside. He was in his element and he wanted to share it with them.

He disappeared inside the stone hut near the fence. He called them to follow. Her eyes took a while to adjust to the dark. It was full of farm implements and cooking utensils. He showed her the cheeses fermenting in muslin in one cool corner. He instructed her to bring the herbs and salt for the soup. He gave a slab of *graviéra* cheese to Alex to take outside.

Andreas added a small handful of dill and salt to the large pot. There was a good draught and the fire burnt up for several minutes and then settled. He reached into a basket and brought out a plastic bottle of his own red wine and a loaf of bread. He handed her a glass as they watched the vegetables simmer. He raised a toast. Lena sat there almost believing that they made some kind of family. Almost believing that they could be happy and that Andreas could stay steady and that his mood wouldn't shift. That she could stay steady. *Yeía mas*, Andreas said. Alex came running from the edge of the field; he had something to show Andreas. He held up a dead mouse by its tail, held it up high for examination. Andreas! he called. He didn't say *Pappoús* in front of her. We should put it back in the earth, said Andreas. Together they went to lay it at the edge of the field, to dig a small hole and cover it with leaves. She poured herself another glass of wine, checking that Andreas couldn't see her. She saw him smoothing the earth at the tiny burial mound, standing back, arms folded, talking with Alex. She watched them walk slowly to the hose pump, still deep in conversation. She saw him take the child's hands and rub them through the water. Andreas smiling. They both walked back shaking out their wet hands. Her son said something that made Andreas laugh out loud.

To the Island

When they were back and sitting by the fire, Andreas pulled the child onto his lap and ran his hand through the boy's hair. He did this unselfconsciously as if it were an everyday event. He seemed happy. *Alex makes him happy*, she thought and for a moment she was heartsore at the ease between them. How quickly they had settled into each other, accepted each other. For her part, she could not let Andreas see the small curled-up self that wanted his acknowledgement. She felt that there was nothing she could do to win him over.

Andreas rubbed the child's neck. And now, we eat!

Alex sat on his grandfather's lap for a minute longer and leant into his chest.

I can hear your heart, he said.

Good, said Andreas, then pushed him off gently, picking up the soup ladle and standing over the black pot. He turned around and smiled, pointed to his chest: This means I am still alive.

*

At night, sometimes from a distance, Lena observed her father's strange ritual with the cupboard. Every night the same. The precision with which Andreas packed and unpacked everything. The care with which he locked the drawer.

One night she couldn't handle it any more.

What are you looking for? she had asked, standing in the doorway. Maybe I can help.

He had looked up as if in a trance. What do you mean?

You lock the drawer. You rearrange the cupboard.

It's nothing, he'd said. *Típota*. Before sleep, I like all to be in order. Don't worry, he'd said, his tone hard. It's nothing.

Kaliníhta, he'd said, closing the cupboard door. He stood with his back to the door, waiting for her to leave, the key to the drawer in his hand.

Kaliníhta, she'd said, resolving not to mention it again. She had backed away and headed downstairs to her room.

Andreas had waited until it was safe for him to continue; his hand shook. When he was sure that Lena was in her room, he'd opened the cupboard again and continued where he left off, rearranging the contents, pushing back the night, putting obstacles in his way.

*

From late March, the sun sparked intermittently. It rained heavily and the fields were green. It was more rain than they'd had for years, everyone agreed. The dams would be full and all the neighbours were happy. The roof leaked again and the downstairs plumbing was bad. The wood around the shutters started peeling. Andreas was busy with all of this. He wanted to whitewash the house before Easter. He did this every year along with all his neighbours. Lena tried to make herself useful. She would go to the hardware store to buy paint or nails or brushes for him, learning how to express herself properly. Andreas would coach her, telling her exactly what to say. She would write it all down and then walk around the house trying to memorize the words to a rhythm, a beat. The way she once memorized whole sequences of steps and gestures. It made Andreas smile, but he hid this from her. Occasionally he would correct her pronunciation, he would be firm. He watched her trip over the words like a child trying to walk and it pained him to see it. The lost child was always lost and he didn't know how to reach her – this adult child standing before him.

Lena felt the full weight of this show: it was hers. She had staged the production. But she didn't know how to move or where to position herself. She was performing the role of daughter with no one to direct her.

In the first weeks of April, there were electrical storms and days when it rained non-stop. It reminded Lena of rain she'd only ever seen in Bali or North Queensland. Heavy wild rain; huge raindrops. After one of these downpours, she opened the door to the veranda a fraction and looked across. A small bird was there, trembling in one corner. She hoped it was the same bird. And if it was an omen, she didn't know what to make of it.

The bird is back! she called out to Andreas and Alex. It's here!

The three of them stood just behind the door, trying to keep quiet, looking over at the bird.

Theé mou, thank God! Andreas said. These past weeks, his old simple life had changed. His orderly life. Of the seasons, of the animals. His routines to keep himself in check. For several winters he'd cared for that bird – in the life before this daughter and this grandson – and each year the bird had come back. It had not perished. It had not been hunted to death. *He had not betrayed its trust.* He felt grateful for that. He couldn't even begin to convey this to Lena or the boy.

The bird connected him to his old life. It would sustain him in some way, long after they were gone.

Theé mou, he said again and went out of the kitchen, whistling to himself.

8

Soon it would be Easter. Andreas opened the weekend paper to see a series of photographs. At first he thought it was an exhibition; most probably in Athens or Thessaloniki. It would be August before anything of real interest came to the island. His mind ran on. The images were beautiful and strange, there was something spectral about them. At first he thought they were X-rays of trees and branches and coral. They seemed to be from landscapes known to him. Natural forms. Then he realized exactly what it was he was looking at. He shut the paper. Got up and moved quickly towards the front door; a sudden shot of adrenaline. It made him want to run. He stood in the doorway. He was alone in the house and aware of the quiet. Alex and Lena were in the *Hóra*. He went back inside and sat again. Opened the paper. Read the captions. The photographs belonged to a German doctor, a renowned professor of medicine. The Professor collected X-rays – ghost images, he called them – of broken bones and hairline fractures. He'd amassed this collection over many years. An inventory of strains and stresses on the body: a nail embedded in a skull; a needle rammed into a spine. X-rays of torture. The professor travelled with this exhibition all over the world to inform and educate, he said.

Torturers have nothing to fear if nothing can be proved, a quote ran along the top of one page. *This work is proof.* Andreas forced himself to look at a kneecapping from Northern Ireland, the limb like a diseased tree with pellets freckling the leg. He turned the page to a photo from Chad – a man's jaw smashed by an electric truncheon. A cropped photo of the blue-white metatarsals of an Iranian girl, elongated, disfigured, the toes clamped by the Revolutionary guard. And so on. And so on. And so on. He took a deep breath and turned over. From Guinea Bissau – dark lines on lower leg bones, austere as a Zen painting. It could be an image of bamboo. He spent a long time looking at this. But it was the final image which got to him. A small black-and-white X-ray from Turkey. The feet of a Kurdish man. Two swollen ankles flattened to light and dark at the toes. He could not see it as human. He turned the newspaper at an angle. Then Andreas understood that this was, in fact, an image of his own feet. *Fálanga.* As if decades had collapsed into an instant, as if time had run backwards, he looked at the photo from Kurdistan and felt a needle-twinge run along his calf and thrum in his right ankle. At night the soles of his feet still pained him. On bad days he walked with effort. He turned the photograph this way and that. He turned the page expecting one final image, hoping for some proof; but no, there were no images from Greece, from forty years before. Only his body carried the memory.

X-rays reveal what the eye cannot see.

Andreas closed the paper and reached for his cigarettes.

He could show this professor some things. His racked feet were only part of it. He took off one boot and looked down at his toes, spread his foot on the floor. He took off his sock and looked again for a comparison with the Kurdish man. Returned to the captions:

Does the age of the injury match the time-frame?

Does the story match the pattern of injury?

He put his sock and boot back on. He got up from the table and opened the cutlery drawer. It was daylight and he felt safe approaching it. He patted the knife handles, reassuring himself that they were still there. Then he took out a pair of scissors and started cutting. He kept cutting until all the photographs were in pieces on the floor, kept cutting and cutting until half of the newspaper was gone; until it lay in shreds at his feet, as if he'd made a nest for himself. He kicked at the piles of paper with his boot. Then he went calmly to the store cupboard and got out the broom.

After the photographs he found it difficult to settle. He called to the dog and walked up into the hills. He walked until he got to the highest point out behind the village, up beyond the telephone masts. He sat looking out over the sea. He sat there with his feet throbbing and the cloud of his thoughts massing down.

Lena and Alex would be back by now.

This daughter and her son. Somehow they'd got in close. Despite his best efforts, they'd got to him. As if he'd put down his armour of years and now the world rushed in. Bright and warm and hard and soft and he was full of feelings he had no name for.

As if the daughter and her boy had come upon him in a closed room and opened the shutters. They'd let in the light and it was too strong. He felt blinded. *And one day soon they would leave.* The thought stabbed at him. It kept stabbing. He'd found himself these past weeks waiting for the boy's voice in the late afternoon. Looking forward to their company after he was back from the fields and the work of the day was done. He'd listen for the rush of small feet on the stairs, for the child's sun to burst through the door and warm through him. He'd wait for this daughter to ask if he wanted coffee; something sweet? The way she moved around the house; the flowers in glass jars, her attempts to please him in small ways. Her faltering Greek. As if she were a child offering up her first words. He would correct her. Sometimes he was too strict, he knew this. He didn't praise her efforts enough. He felt overwhelmed, as if he were truly a father showing her the everyday miracles of the world, the nouns and the verbs she'd missed out on. Naming things as he went. *Apple. Cup. Life. Death.* Even the simplest of words that she'd learnt long ago, she would repeat after him. And when she held the words up to the light the world rushed in. He had no defences. He was too old for tenderness. He was a stranger to himself; undone by the thought that they had swept into his life and would soon leave. He wiped at his eyes. They'd cracked him like a seed and he lay there exposed and uncertain. They brought rain and sun. They would take the sun and the rain with them. And he would stay on in his old life, as if they had never come to the island. He would stay on.

He could no longer imagine what this would mean.

He tried to come up with a plan. He felt heavy and disconsolate. He would later say to himself: *It started then.* But of course it started before. It started the moment he saw the daughter at the edge of the field, bicycle against the fence. It started the first time he saw the grandson asleep, watching his breath rise and fall, and bent down to smooth the blankets about him. He'd been cracked open. Now, everywhere, beneath the beauty of the world, all he could see were X-rays of pain.

The dog was off chasing rabbits and he called to the dog, too harshly. They made their way down the path to the village.

When he got in it was early evening, already dark. Lena gave him a strange look. We were worried, she said. Each time she returned to the house and he wasn't there it triggered some old response. As if she knew in her bones he would always desert her.

Marsoula rang, she said. Left a message with Kiria Sofia. She's invited us to stay with her. After Easter.

Good idea, he said. You must go.

You can come with us, said Alex.

She will come here for Easter? Andreas changed the subject.

Yes, said Lena. They'd all been invited to the neighbours' for Easter Sunday.

Kalá, said Andreas.

We could go back with Marsoula after, said Lena.

You can come with us! Alex tried again.

No. No. I have work here, Andreas said. Conscious that after Easter, after their stay with Marsoula, they would be leaving.

Well, said Lena. Of course we can go by ourselves . . .

It will be good for Marsoula. He was speaking too fast. And good for you too. A plan was forming. He needed time to prepare for his old life of solitude, his life before they came. And here is a little boring maybe? But with your aunt, in the mountains . . .

We're not bored, said Lena, wanting to reassure him. Are we, Alex?

No, said Alex. He knew that this was what his mother wanted to hear. Although there were times when he *was* bored, and he thought the mountains might be good. But only if his grandfather could come with them.

I will ring her, said Andreas, taking the phone card from his wallet. I will ring her *amésos*.

Lena wondered what was going through his head. He was so difficult to second guess. His sudden moods, the way he withdrew.

He wants us to go, said Alex matter-of-factly, watching Andreas walk down the stairs, down the path to the phone box. He wants to be by himself.

It's not that.

He's used to it, Alex repeated. He's not used to us.

Maybe, she said, too sharply. Or maybe it's something else. Nothing to do with us.

They waited for Andreas to return. He came up the path, whistling.

It is all decided, he said, without looking at them directly. You will go to Marsoula.

*

186

It was *Megáli Evdomáda*, the big week before Easter. All the neighbours were fasting and Andreas also fasted although he rarely went to church. He ate no meat, nothing with oil. He did not drink. He refused sugar in his coffee.

Lena didn't understand. But if you don't go to church ...

It's the good discipline, he shrugged. But he fasted for other reasons. To be part of something bigger than himself. To be at home here on the island. He fasted out of respect for his neighbours. Once or twice he had gone at midnight on Easter Saturday to hear the bells, even though he didn't believe. Suffering, death, the betrayal of the Christ; the days of mourning pressed down. The people gone from him. *Irini gone from him*. No one returned.

He did not think that he could go to the church this year – not with Lena and Alex. He did not think he could bear it.

It was Good Friday. The air was warm and fragrant and there was the bleating of goats and lambs. The animals could sense what was coming, Lena thought. The lambs clustered at the edge of the fields. The honeysuckle was out. The jasmine fully flowered. Lena and Alex and Marsoula walked down into the *Hóra*. All the shops had shut early and there was a silence over the island, as if a great tragedy had struck. As if everyone were attending a funeral. Andreas stayed at home. He felt tense. He tried to read the newspaper but it was impossible. *The nails in hands and feet. The expression on the face of the Christ*. He did not need to witness such suffering. Every year he found it difficult. In the early evening, Lena and Alex waited with Marsoula for the procession of the *Epitáfios* from the main church. The priest and the bishops, all the people dressed up, hands cupped around candles. The solemn faces and the beauty of the songs, the funeral laments – the call and response. The funeral bier covered in flowers and candles shouldered by men in dark suits. The sense of expectancy and tension. The build-up to something of wonder and release.

Back in the village, Andreas called to the dog and walked up into the mountains until his legs ached and night fell and he could be fully certain that the danger inside himself had passed.

*

The next evening, Easter Saturday, Lena and Alex went with Marsoula to the village church. The mood was lighter, everyone waiting for midnight. It took three men to ring the bells, holding the thick heavy rope. Kirios Giannis was one of them; he gripped the cords in his strong hands and leant back, as if pulling at a ship's sail. The bells rang and people called out:

Christós Anésti! Christ is risen!

Alithós Anésti! Truly risen!

The bells kept ringing. Children threw bangers and let off firecrackers. There was smoke everywhere. The noise was incredible, after nearly two days of silence. A celebration! Some of the villagers had tears in their eyes, relief that this time of mourning was over. The Christ had risen. A new year had begun. The children were clean and glossy-haired. Alex lit firecrackers too. He was excited to be up so late with so many people, so much colour and commotion.

They made their way down the path from the church trying to keep their candles lit. Andreas met them at the door. He had stayed at home, as he promised himself. It would be too much for him to attend a celebration with this new family. He no longer had a grip on his emotions. He paced the house, waiting for them to return, and his eyes filled when he saw them with their candles. He lifted Alex up so that he could make the sign of the cross at the lintel – a burnt black cross that would stay until next Easter. Andreas had a sudden painful thought – next Easter he would be alone. Next Easter, the daughter and the boy would not be with him.

This cross will keep us safe, he said. It will bring light for another year.

Is that why you do it? Lena asked.

Yes, he said. To bring light. We Greeks do this. He seemed sad, Lena thought.

Andreas hoped that the cross would be a talisman for him; to keep him safe. To keep them all safe. He wished he could be certain of such comfort.

They sat down just after midnight to break the fast with *mayeirítsa*, the goat's head soup that Andreas had made. The next morning everyone was up preparing for the feast; the smell of grilled meat and smoke carried all over the village. Andreas always had Easter with Kiria Maria and Giannis. Marsoula usually came down from Apeira to join them. They would sit out at a big table in the street, set out under the plane trees. People from the village always dropped by to give good wishes. *Hrónia Pollá!*

Lena watched Andreas carefully. He seemed subdued. He saw her watching him and held up his glass. *Xrónia Pollá*, he said and smiled a tight smile. He pushed a plate of lamb towards her. Eat, he said. He thought that she was looking better these past weeks. More colour. Less drawn. He wanted her to be well. He did not mention her operation, but in his own way, he tried to take care of her. To tell her to rest. Eat, he said again. He sat at one end of the table opposite Kirios Giannis, as if this were his accustomed place, a father with his family. As if his life had always been like this; as if he had never known anything different.

*

On the Tuesday after Easter, Lena and Alex left for Apeira.

Andreas felt in high spirits driving them down to the port. He stood with them but the bus was late and the longer they waited the more his feelings confounded him. The child tugged at his hand, tugged at his heart, asking him to change his mind, to come with them. Andreas kept saying no, it wasn't possible. *Pappoús! Please*. Alex didn't look at his mother when he said the Greek word. He knew the effect that it would have on her. But it was the effect on Andreas which he noted. The word gripped Andreas and would not let go. As if in the naming he had a new place in the world – tethered to this small insistent person. Alex kept waving until the bus was out of sight. Andreas stood there waving until he knew he must seem foolish. But the child expected it and he got pleasure from making him happy. He had observed the way Lena and Alex waved goodbye until one of them was out of sight. He stood looking after the bus, shaking out his hands, and looked around, self-conscious. *He must return to his work.* When he got back to the field he picked up his spade and kept digging long after the sun went down. He did not stop for *mesimerianó*. There was no one to share it with. No one to cook for. He kept digging as if he had a guard at his back, a gun at his ribs, forcing him on. He kept digging through to his old life, before this daughter and this grandson; as if he were trying to excavate himself. The earth was hard and it was hard work. For the first time in two months he returned to a dark house. He hesitated at the threshold. He hesitated at the edge of his old life. He turned on the balcony light and opened the door. Darkness pushed back at him. The place was empty as a cave. He walked into the study and there was the sight of a small shoe, a small sock. An upturned toy truck with three wheels. He looked around for the other wheel. I must fix it, he thought, before the boy returns.

For three days and nights this went on. He would come back from the fields to the dark house. He would walk through the empty rooms. His old life echoing back. He longed to hear the child's voice. He longed to hear Lena's accented Greek, making him smile, making her laugh when he corrected her. *Haliá* for *hália*. *Carpets* instead of *terrible*! Where to put the stress? She always forgot. How many times had he told her? He couldn't bring himself to go down to the telephone box to ring them. His card had expired and he couldn't bring himself to buy a new one. He sat there in the evenings with the dog at his feet, unable to read, unable to breathe properly. He sat there with the toy truck spread out on the table, a screwdriver in hand, unable to put the pieces back together. He did not cook. He hardly ate. He had no appetite.

On the fourth night, old Kiria Sofia came to the door to tell him that they'd left a message. They would stay a little longer. They would be back next week.

What? Andreas felt bereft and tried to calm himself. Which day?

She gestured around the balcony with her stick. Why are you sitting in the dark, Andreas?

He tried to think of some excuse. I'm resting, he said. My eyes are sore. And then he asked again, Which day?

Next week, repeated Kiria Sofia. They did not say when.

Edáksi, he said. All right. Though the situation was far from all right.

He sat there in the dark with the toy truck in pieces about him. He put his head in his hands, listening to Kiria Sofia tap her way downstairs, across the street to her lighted house, to the son who was waiting for her and to her daughters who visited every day. To the family she had always known.

*

He tried to keep himself busy but there was one task he'd avoided. It was a small task but it demanded a lot from him. He had to renew his truck licence. Tomorrow he would do it. But tomorrow came and went and he couldn't force himself. He had to be strong to go to the police station. Every day he felt less strong.

The daughter and grandson had been away for a week when he finally drove down to the port. He parked near the police station and went in to sit on a hard bench in the waiting room, his old licence in his back pocket. All around were arguments and raised voices. A man and his son were in dispute with the *Dímos*. The son threw his large hessian sack full of cheese in the middle of the room. *Graviéra, mízíthra, anthótiro.* The boy called the names of the cheeses, extolling their quality. It would go to court, he heard a young policeman say. Of course it would go to court. Selling unpasteurized cheese! Selling cheese on the street, like the gypsy! This is Europe, the policeman said. You're not in the village now.

Just then the door opened and a tall man stooped through. The police chief. Andreas caught him in profile. He had only ever seen the man at a distance. He waited for the man to speak and his hands shook as he bent over his shoes pretending to tie first one shoelace and then another. *Something familiar.* Andreas sat there gripping his old licence. An iron taste in his mouth. The smell of bleach at his back.

Andreas kept looking at his shoes. The police chief was at the counter.

Captain Spiro. *Kalá íste?* the young policeman said.

Mia hará, said the police chief. Andreas could hear him quite clearly. It occurred to him that the voice was not quite the same. A small doubt that he chose to ignore.

I can count on you?

Málista! Of course! the young policeman said. You have my vote.

The police chief slapped his hand on the front counter. Bravo!

The new police chief came from Athens. He'd been on the island a few months. Andreas at first paid him no attention until one day he saw him walking along the *paralía*. *Something about the walk*. The police chief was a little stooped, a little paunched, hair greying at the sides, still young. *Could it be?* From then on the police chief insinuated himself into dreams and into thought-crevices. Andreas rubbed at his sore wrists and ankles and his nights became even more troubled.

Andreas wondered if he could get up now and walk out. He wanted desperately to walk out. He hoped that his name would not be called.

What happened to people after the Junta?

Lena had asked him this question. Already he was thinking of this daughter and grandson in the past.

Some people thrived, he said. Grew fat. Continued on.

No one went to jail?

The big fishes, he said. There was a trial. Only the big fishes got caught.

Andreas had long dreamed of what he would do, if he were certain, if it were possible. What he would do if he ever saw one of the men from the room in Athens: the room of the bench and the rope. He had not counted on the man from the camp.

The police chief disappeared into a back room with the sack

of cheese. Andreas was directed to the counter. He paid for the new licence and gave a little more in an envelope to smooth things. He made it back to his truck and put the key in the ignition. He eased out into the road just as the police chief emerged from the station and started crossing the street. Without thinking, Andreas accelerated, making straight for him. The police chief moved slowly like a large animal, sure of its own power.

It would be so easy. It would be an accident. It would be done.

At the last minute, Andreas braked hard and then they were face to face. The police chief cursed and slammed the grille of the truck. Andreas stared him down. He thought he saw a flicker in the man's eyes: a prison camp and barbed wire and the sea beyond that. It splintered in front of him. Then the police chief blinked and cursed and slammed the truck once more and moved on.

Andreas pulled to the side of the road, breathing heavily, and lit a cigarette. His hands trembled. He was getting old. Starting to see reflections that weren't there. Imagining things.

He had been mistaken. He had the wrong man.

*

That night the old dream wakes him. It is always the same:

A man in uniform comes to the door and calls for him, Adonis.

I am not Adonis.

The man holds up a form and points to the name.

A mistake.

The man lets the paper fall. He steps forward and stabs Andreas in the chest with his index finger. The man reaches right through. *It's all mistakes*, the man says. *You can't change the world. Washington, Moscow. Left and Right. The world is fixed.* There is a wrench in the chest. The man stands there with Andreas' heart in his fist.

Andreas jolts up. One hand to his heart. His chest sore. His pulse riots in his neck, his arms. He thinks he is back on the prison island. His hands feel heavy. The world has changed. Washington. Moscow. All different.

Only Andreas has not changed. Only Andreas is not different.

He feels a pain around his heart. He tells himself it is not real. It is only the dream. These days more and more he has pain that is not physical and feelings he has no name for.

Cut through it.

If the pain goes, what then?

He thinks of his grandson. He has taken to sitting with the boy and reading to him in the evenings. First a story in Greek and then in English. The boy leaning against his chest. Waiting for the boy to close his eyes and fall asleep. Lately he wakes in the middle of the night and moves to the study door and stands there a while, to check that the boy is still breathing.

He thinks of the daughter: so wary, so direct, so much himself. He wants to ease her sadness and doesn't know how.

This lost-and-found-thread of family. Only now it comes to him with the force of argument that his life could have been very different. Overwhelmingly his life had led in one direction: not to be a father, not to be a grandfather. To live alone. To live an ordered life. To keep the terrors in check. He thought he was one thing and that life would continue on as it always had. *Now this.*

He wants his feet to ache, his neck to hurt, his limbs to shatter.

To check if his grandson is sleeping. To ease the sadness of this daughter.

This is pain, he tells himself. True pain he has kept at a distance all these years. The world of ordinary everyday feeling. And who is he not to feel it? Who is he not to endure it?

He makes his way to the store cupboard. He takes out the broom and the dustpan. He removes the cleaning liquids and the olive oil. The secateurs, the gardening gloves, the compost and the candles. Glass bottles. Boxes and cartons. He feels for the key under the hessian sack in the corner. He disrupts the careful order of the cupboard.

He disrupts the careful order of his life, searching for the key.

Makrónisos, February 1968

The door scrapes open and the guard puts the key in his pocket.

The professor blinks into the light and leaves in an army transport along with other prisoners. At intervals from Athens, through the grille over the windows he sees billboards: 'Greece is Risen', 'Greece of the Christian Greeks' and 'Coca-Cola'. He sees rows of orange buttons for sale at the kiosks. Small circles of orange with a grin. At first he thinks it is some kind of protest. Some kind of joke. There are stickers with the same fake grin in shop windows as they pass. At intersections he sees suited men with the orange buttons in their lapels. The Americans bring new fads and fizzy drinks and military aid. Keep smiling. *His bruised mind tries hard to make the connections. After these months in prison, after interrogation, he can no longer concentrate properly. He closes his eyes and sees an American grin on a lapel. He knows there will be no smiling at his destination.*

Makrónisos. This is where they are headed. A small bleak island in the middle of the sea. The nearest land is Kea but the currents are so rough you could drown trying to get there. The prisoners know this.

At the port of Lavrio they're loaded onto an old army boat.

To the Island

Out on deck he hunches into himself, feels everything tighten. Makrónisos. *As the island comes into view he feels pain in his feet, in his neck, in his arms. All the places which pain him. From this angle, the island is a drowned animal with an elongated tail.* Makrónisos. Long Island. *He could walk it in an hour if his legs were up to it. If he were free to walk that far.*

He suddenly longs for Irini. In prison, word came that she was in hiding. Unable to make contact. Looking out to sea he imagines himself in his old life, at home with his books, listening to music, waiting for her knock at his door.

Here, he will not have his own door. Here, there will be nothing of his old life.

The first weeks on the island pass. The professor reads and walks. He reads books left by other prisoners: copies of Aristophanes and Sophocles recently banned from the National Theatre. So far they have survived here, escaped notice. He recites dates and place names to keep his mind busy. He recites poetry to himself. Over and over he recites lines he has made his own. Lines that will not let him go. He picks up a stick and carves words into the dry earth:

κανένας δεν κρατάει τα κλειδιά του
no-one holds his own keys

He translates into English for himself and then into French. He keeps his mind busy.

One grey day a young man approaches and asks for a cigarette.

He is not much more than a boy. He could be one of my students, thinks the professor.

It was beautiful here once. The young man makes an arc with the cigarette.

He has a low deep voice. The voice of an actor, perhaps. The professor ignores the boy. He smokes his cigarette staring out through the barbed wire at the sea rising and falling.

Eleni of Troy. She came here.

Yes. The professor is brusque. He wants to smoke in silence, but the boy keeps talking. It was never beautiful, he interrupts the boy. Nothing grows here. Nothing ever will.

The young man changes tack. He looks sidelong at the professor. You read a lot.

The professor is immediately on high alert; as if someone has pulled a switch inside. I read when I can. He reads books passed around. The copy of Ritsos his sister sent, disguised with a plain cover.

The boy sees him tense: Trust me, he says, I like the books myself. Ta mátia sou dekatéssera, he says, tapping the side of his nose and looking around. Who to trust? The boy laughs.

I taught history, says the professor, standing a little straighter, as if the past still meant something. My life was books.

I'm interested in the history, says the boy. He could be on the radio. A voice which draws you in. Later the professor will come to think of him as Satan: a serpent hissing in his ear.

I study literature. The young man does not use the past tense, the professor notes this. He does not speak of his life before. Here we could fill a university, the boy continues. So many students, so many professors! There is energy in the way he moves and speaks. He is full of gestures. He takes long steps around the camp. There is nothing broken or diminished about him. Why is this young man so much himself? *The professor, by contrast, is no longer sure where he ends and another human begins. He knows that he could fracture and fall at any moment and that people would step over and around him or grind him to dust. He experiences the world now as a closed eye, a turned back. The world as a truncheon or a knife or an iron bar. And yet what he feels pulsing from the boy is precisely a kind of trust from a time before. Something he once shared: a trust in* filoxenía. *In human warmth and kindness.*

What are you reading? There, the words are out. Despite himself, the professor asks the first real question he's asked anyone since he came here. Since he got out of his cell in Athens. The first question that has not been about survival, only: where to sleep, where to lay his boots, where is the latrine? It is the first question that connects him to his old life.

The boy jingles the telephone tokens in his pocket.

Lampedusa, he says. Chekhov . . .

The professor clicks his tongue, suspicious. The banned books. Of course he would give such an answer . . .

The boy says quickly: With different covers. Religious covers. He draws on his cigarette. And you read Ritsos . . .

The professor turns to look directly at him now. The young man is tall and thin with green eyes and black hair. A

*good-looking boy. With that voice and that face – the thought
persists – the man could be an actor. Perhaps he is acting now?
The professor squints into the distance, puts a hand up to his eyes
as if to ward off a blow.*

*It's my own business, says the professor, his voice hard. He
does not say that history has failed him and that only a poet gets
under the skin of fact.*

*The young man laughs. I'm curious only, Professor! I mean
you no harm. He pauses. The professor stays silent and wills him
to leave but the young man is persistent. I'm here because they
found leaflets – not even my leaflets. The boy glances over at the
face set against him and takes a gamble. And you, Professor?*

Ti?

You are here . . .? The boy leaves the question hanging.

*It's my business, the professor angles himself away. He does not
say that he could be here for any number of reasons; some of them
true. Then the thought of telling his story – the possibility of
relief – suddenly rains through him. To start from the beginning.
He feels as if he could burst and flood with the telling. Of what
happened to him in prison. But just in time he dams the flood
of himself.*

It's a long story, he says.

*The young man shrugs. In this place, all our stories are long.
He puts out his hand. My name is Vasilis.*

*The professor stubs out his cigarette and does not extend his
hand. He traces a line in the dirt with his foot. He has kept to
himself since he came here. He no longer trusts human contact;*

he no longer knows how to judge a person. He realizes he can no longer distinguish between the hand of friendship and the clenched fist.

Héro polí, says the professor. Pleased to meet you, he says to himself, turning on his heel and walking back the way he has come.

*

You are here . . . ?

It's a long story.

On his makeshift bed, the professor replays the conversation looking for clues. The island is full of hafiés. *Everyone knows this. The camp is full of informers and spies. The Colonels have built a nation of informers and spies.*

I'm interested in the history, said the young man.

The professor, lying in his bed, scratching at his insect bites, feels suddenly curious. After that first encounter it seems that wherever he is in the camp the young man seeks him out, drawing him in with that voice, that easy manner. The professor does not ask too many questions. Does not give too much away. It is time to put the young man to the test.

You said you like the history, the professor asks one day. He wants to interrogate the boy. What history?

The young man is not thrown off. Our history. The history of this place. What they did to our comrades. How one thing lead to another. This is important, no?

The professor concedes that yes, this is important.

Vasilis smiles. His smile is genuine: it starts with his eyes. My grandfather was sent here, he continues. He points to the remains of a low building. In D Battalion. Over there. See the fence? Shall we look?

The professor, intrigued, decides to look.

There were 500 men here. Fourteen to a tent. Vasilis paces around the stumps of the fence. Kept separate from the other prisoners. My grandfather was here for two years. Until the end of the Civil War. Battalion D. They were beaten and tortured. With bamboo, with iron bars. Their spines broken. My grandfather – blinded in one eye. The torture. He looks sideways at Andreas. Here it was the worst.

The professor looks at the ruins of D Battalion and folds his arms tight across his chest.

You too?

The professor keeps silent.

Until now, I've been lucky, says Vasilis. No beatings. Nothing. He crosses himself from right to left and looks up at the sky. Theé mou! But my grandfather. He was not so fortunate. He was the tormented soul. Vasilis picks up a stone and aims at the further limits of the fence. He launches the stone. Under torture, the things a man will say . . .

The professor feels his limbs go heavy as he watches the stone hit its target and sees the stone shatter and fall. He rubs at his arms, rolls his shirtsleeves down. I must go back now, he says.

*

On the island there is always the threat of time. In winter months on a day without sun, the hours pour down. The sea is not seamed at the horizon. It's a world without boundaries – how to mark such a day? Everything loosens under its weight. The grip of the camp slackens. The sea and the sky are one. The jailers and the prisoners are one. Everyone feels it. The professor feels it. Everyone waits for something to happen. In the quiet of such times, with a flat sea and everything flat, nothing to hold on to, with a grey horizon and a grey sky, men take their own life.

After a week of five suicides, the professor considers the prospect himself.

Always he'd thought it a sign of weakness. But here, anything seems possible. Here on the island, in winter, all dark thoughts converge. There is only the flat sea and the flat sky and the absence of light; the island of Kea so far and so close. The wild currents in between. Here there are only the night sweats and the bad dreams and the pull of unnumbered days.

The professor sees two guards drag a blanket past a row of prisoners. The face in the blanket is covered but wrists hang down, scraping blood in the dirt. Another blanket goes past; the face uncovered. The professor notes the noose marks at the throat and returns to his digging as if he has registered a dead dog or cat. Something not of the same species. Something separate.

Vasilis is at his side. He stops work to look as the bodies are dragged out of the camp.

Where do they take them?

The lucky ones?

Vasilis spits in the dirt. The revolutionary duty is to stay alive.

I'm no revolutionary.

Then, quite unexpectedly, Vasilis turns on him: Did you sign?

The professor hears an edge to the voice and sidesteps the question. I didn't sign, the professor says. He knows well the behaviour of fanatic Party members. Vasilis wants to know if he signed a statement denouncing communism.

You were the lucky one! The young man's voice turns bitter.

The professor senses that a dangerous moment has not quite passed.

What did you tell them? Vasilis asks outright. A great boulder splits under the force of his axe. What did they want you to say?

I didn't say nothing. The professor takes a deep breath. His nights are full of what he almost said. Of what he didn't say. His nights are full of what would have happened, if he had not lost consciousness, if he had not gone under.

That's not what I've heard.

The professor's heart constricts and he adjusts the grip on his shovel. You hear many things. Not all of them true.

Vasilis gives a short odd laugh. Listen. He looks around to make sure they are alone. They forced me to sign. They forced me to give names.

Names?

We both know, Professor, that torture begins with interrogation. I'm not a brave man. Vasilis sounds a lot older all of a sudden, as if he has endured too much. It's a revolutionary duty to stay alive. He repeats this and gives another odd laugh. The end justifies the means, my friend. *He pauses.* My ends, my means.

You call yourself a communist? The professor shakes his head.

Some names are expendable.

At this, the professor puts down his shovel: There are no names worth telling, he says. He knows this is not true, but he wants to believe it. He tries to forget the name of Stavros. How close he came to giving this name among many: he had thought this boy was Irini's lover. He had thought many things. He gives an involuntary shudder.

Vasilis stops digging. You look troubled, my friend. He puts a hand on the older man's shoulder. I hear your shouts in the night . . .

In the night? The professor flushes red. His whole body red at the thought.

Vasilis looks at him. The camp is full of shouts in the night. He calculates his next step. A woman's name . . .

The professor looks away and wipes his brow with the back of his hand. Calms himself.

There is always a woman, Vasilis soothes.

The professor wants to say her name. He misses her. He longs for her. Then other, darker feelings surface: irrationally, he blames her for his suffering. He is in prison here and where is she? He has heard nothing from her. She may be in hiding, this he has heard. But he imagines that she is with some other man. He imagines her, safe, warm, the bourgeois radical protected by her big family. Her big right-wing family. How easy for her to take risks. He becomes angry with Irini and his grip on himself loosens, like his grip on the day. As if there are no boundaries anymore.

Vasilis leans on his shovel, gives the professor his full attention. She was a comrade? He pushes a little, who knows what he may find. He pushes again. In November there had been a trial, but not all terrorists were caught. He persists, From the Patriotic Front?

The professor hesitates. Who knew what groups Irini was involved in? She'd become more extreme. More secretive, since the death of Mandilaras. He nods.

Vasilis whistles through his teeth.

Irini. The professor says her name and feels as if he is split in half. He wants to let go, he wants to hold tight. He could tell this man everything he knows

You gave her name? says Vasilis, his voice low.

No. No. I didn't give her name.

Where is she now?

In hiding.

Irini. Vasilis repeats her name.

The professor nods. A student. But I didn't give her name . . .

You gave another?

No. The professor stays silent.

Vasilis changes tack. Trusts his instincts. And her family?

The professor's memories are shot. He gathers himself. She comes from a big family. A family of the Right. The words spool out.

Vasilis takes a step back. As if the family name of this woman *is the last name he would be interested in.*

The professor wonders if he calls her name in his sleep for comfort or for some other reason. His voice suddenly cracks. She was having an affair. She broke with me . . .

From a big family? Vasilis stays steady.

Very big.

Vasilis throws out some well-known family names.

No. No. Of course not. The professor shakes his head. None of those . . .

Well?

The professor looks at him. It seems at that moment he cannot see the eyes of Vasilis. It's as if he is staring into a hard sun.

He says her last name.

No. I don't know it. Vasilis shrugs.

She has relatives in the Junta. The Minister for Justice . . .

No. Vasilis shakes his head. Keeps his head down. I don't know this name.

She worked with Mandilaras . . .

The lawyer of Papandreou. The murdered lawyer. One name leads to another. Vasilis nods, struggling to remain in the present, not to leap to a future of honours and promotions. Mandilaras, he says, lowering his voice. He thinks of the lawyer's body washed up on Rhodos. He was a good man.

Kalópsychos, echoes the professor.

A large gull flies over as they make their way back to camp. It makes a lonely desperate sound.

Vasilis puts his hand on the older man's shoulder. And you,

Professor — never forget this — you, too, are kalópsychos.

*

The next morning when the professor wakes the first thing he notices is the light. It is a new day; the sun breaks through. He feels as if he has put down a burden. *For the first time in months he is not alone. He goes looking for Vasilis.*

All that day and the next the professor trawls the camp looking for his friend. For this is what Vasilis has become.

Have you seen my friend?

His fellow prisoners shrug and go back to their távli *and their covert lessons on dialectical materialism.*

Vasilis? They shake their heads. No one has seen him.

The days pass and the skies darken into spring. The professor can no longer tell one day from another. More blankets are carried from the camp. The professor checks each face carefully.

He notes the outline of Kea — so close, so far — a trick of the light. He waits. As if he were a fish at the mercy of the waves and the wind. A small fish caught in a vast sea net. He writes Irini's name in the dirt. He calls her name, over and over. He cannot trust himself. No one is safe around him. If he can say her name, he can say anything. He is capable of anything. After more days like this — who knows how many days? — he takes a blunt and rusted knife, the only knife he can find and starts cutting at the net of himself. He cuts right through to muscle and sinew and bone. He starts at the wrists, determined, trying to cut his way through.

The Leaving

9

They caught a taxi from Apeira to the village and it was evening by the time they arrived. The wind was up and there was a power cut. The tail-end of a storm. The street lights were out as they struggled up the stairs and into the house. Marsoula carried a large bag of cheese and olives and bread. She'd packed Tupperware full of spanakopita. Lena tried to persuade her to leave the food, telling her not to worry. They should go quickly. It was an emergency. But Marsoula refused. Lena noted how the older Greeks fixated on food as if the lean times could return. As if starvation lay around the next corner. As they walked up the stairs of her father's house it seemed to her that they were all limping. Alex was too heavy to lift, too old to lift, but with the news of his grandfather it was as if he'd gone back to being an infant, wanting to be held close. He clung to her arm and would not let go.

The house still smelt of cigarette smoke: everything just as he'd left it. The dishes stacked and the floor scrubbed. Lena went around opening up the shutters and windows, briefly letting the air wash through.

Marsoula stood out on the balcony, waiting for Giorgos and

his mother to arrive. Lena heard Kiria Sofia's cane tapping up the stairs. Giorgos with a storm lantern in one hand, throwing huge shadows against the rubber leaves.

They found him on his bed, fully clothed, lying there, Giorgos said. His mother had entered the room first. Giorgos had returned from the fields late afternoon and the shutters of Andreas were closed. But everyone knew that the shutters of Andreas always opened early. Perhaps Andreas is ill? He called to his mother and together they went up to the house, calling, Andreas! Andreas! But no answer. And then they found the door open. Andreas lying there. It was a shock, Kiria Sofia said. A big shock! He was so healthy, she continued. He walked into the *Hóra* every day. Always working in the fields. He swam in the sea all through summer, even some days in winter. He had not seen a doctor in thirty years. Lena listened closely to all this, absorbing the things she didn't know about her father. In an aside to Marsoula, Kiria Sofia said: These days, he did not seem unhappy.

Giorgos interrupted: He is in the clinic now, in the *Hóra*.

His heart? Lena asked.

Giorgos looked anxiously at his mother and then at Marsoula.

He will get better, he said.

Lena looked around for Marsoula but she'd gone back into the kitchen. She could hear Kiria Sofia's voice: We cleaned the room, the sheets, everything . . .

Thank you, said Marsoula.

He is in the clinic now, Giorgos repeated, backing out of the

room. You can ring the doctor tomorrow. He was so tall he had
to bend a little in the doorway.

In the kitchen, the two women looked pale and stricken.
Giorgos nodded good night then gripped his mother by the
elbow and steered her down the steps and out into the dark. The
storm lantern made wave patterns on the leaves and on the
ground, making the smallest thing seem huge.

The door to the main bedroom was ajar and Lena went in and
walked around. She opened the shutters and looked out at the
raddled sky. It was dark and quiet now except for the wind. The
room smelt of disinfectant and the bed had been freshly made.
She sat down on the bed and felt such a mixture of things that she
didn't know how to feel. She was tired, bone-tired, but her mind
was espresso-alert. On the bedside table was a bundle wrapped in
a handkerchief. She unwrapped the bundle: cigarettes; an old
lighter; a leather wallet; three small white stones; a set of keys
with a blue eye key ring. A folded water bill from the *Dímos*.
Andreas had written a note of apology for this unpaid bill, though
everything else was in place, the note said. He had not written
anything else.

Alex had shadowed her quietly and was rubbing his eyes. Now
she walked him to the bed in the study and tucked him in.

Back in the kitchen she saw the dark shape of her aunt over
near the sink.

Where are the candles? Marsoula asked.

It's OK, said Lena. I'll get them. The store cupboard was open.
She tripped on a large stone just inside the door. She tried to get

to the shelves, but her way was blocked. She'd never seen the cupboard like this – the mop and the broom, the bucket and the tins of oil – everything out of place. A torn hessian sack flung over a box and broken glass underfoot. She couldn't find the candles. It was as if someone had come in here in a frenzy.

What's wrong? Marsoula called out.

No candles, said Lena, backing out of the cupboard. It's a mess. She tried to remember where the gas burner was kept.

A mess? Marsoula knew that this was unusual. Andreas kept everything in order.

I'll clean up tomorrow, said Lena. She put a hand on her aunt's shoulder. Don't worry.

Her eyes became more accustomed to the dark. From under the sink she located the small *bríki* Andreas used for coffee and filled it with water. She wanted to make tea and she knew where Andreas kept his chamomile. She remembered where to find the gas burner and the matches next to it. She noticed that one of the drawers was open. The key was still in the lock. She opened it out fully while waiting for the water to boil – it was the cutlery drawer – knives and forks all jumbled. She pushed the drawer shut with her hip.

She sat with Marsoula at the kitchen table. In the dark all they could hear was the cockerel and the donkey and the wind from the sea.

You told me it was his heart, said Lena.

Marsoula sighed. He's safe now. He will come home. He will get better.

Lena could tell that her aunt didn't want to talk, but pressed on. What happened?

It's not the first time . . .

Marsoula . . .

He's not a happy man . . .

You can tell me . . .

But Marsoula moved to the sink to rinse her cup. I'm tired, she said. We'll talk tomorrow.

OK, Lena sighed. Tomorrow.

She drank her tea and then made her way downstairs holding onto Marsoula's arm, guiding her down. This is your room, Lena said. I'll sleep upstairs. She went back up to the study and lay down next to her son and listened to lightning crack again overhead and the light strafing the shutters; the way the thunder shook the mountains, and pulled the sheets tight in around them.

*

Lena slept through the church bells, though they'd rung in her dreams. She threw open the shutters and saw that the storm had passed. The sun was warm and the day was clear. She flicked the light switch and saw that the power was back on.

She saw Marsoula in conversation with Kiria Maria and Kirios Giannis, all of them looking back towards the house. She went into the study to wake her son and kissed his forehead. Time to get up, she said.

She thought of Andreas with a sharp pang. They had the

number of the clinic. They would ring and then go down to the *Hóra*. First, she waited for her aunt to return.

Marsoula came back in with the water canisters and filled the *bríki* for coffee. Sit down, she said to Lena. I have something to tell.

*

Lena sat there listening to Marsoula and felt as if she might never get up again. She closed her eyes and brought her hands up to her face.

Once before, this happened, Marsoula went on, moving around the kitchen, pouring out the coffee into small cups. Many years before. In the prison camp. Long before he came here.

But why now?

It's no one's fault, Marsoula said firmly. He found a daughter and a grandson. He cares for you . . .

He said that?

Andreas never says. Marsoula's tone was sharp. Don't wait for his words, Lena. You will wait a long time.

But I don't understand.

For some people – Marsoula paused – happiness is difficult. Happiness hurts.

It hurts? Lena thought she had misheard or mistranslated.

You get the taste for happiness, said Marsoula. But only sadness is for certain. She turned to face Lena. Some people want only the certain thing.

*

Marsoula went down to ring the clinic and instructed Lena to get clean sheets and pillowcases. She told her to pack all the food they'd brought into a large basket.

When she came back from the phone box she said, Let's go.

Now? But when are the visiting hours?

Marsoula rolled her eyes. They told me to come now. She organized their trip to Andreas as if they were going on a long journey. She put money in an envelope for the doctor.

But why are we taking all this?

We have to, said Marsoula. You have no idea. In the hospital, he will starve. He will have no one to look after him.

Lena helped with the food and with the sheets, found clean pyjamas, soap, and Andreas' wash bag. She called Alex. They crammed into a taxi and Marsoula sat next to the driver. Technically it was the hospital now, Marsoula explained to Lena over her shoulder. No longer a clinic. But there was no surgeon and no one to work the new X-ray machine. Women still went to Athens to birth their babies. Anything bad and people still went to Athens or Siros. There were visiting doctors and only two nurses. Family must change the sheets and bring the food, she said.

When they got to the clinic, the double doors swung open and they walked past a man attached to a drip, smoking in the corridor. Another man lay in a trolley bed further along. Alex clutched the pillows as if they were a life raft. Lena carried the sheets. Marsoula took charge of the food basket. *We look like refugees,* thought Lena. The receptionist told them where to find

Andreas. A foreigner walked through, drunk, covered in glass and the two nurses rushed to his side.

Marsoula pulled back the curtain. Andreas seemed small and thin propped up against the pillows, his eyes shut. He had a drip in one arm and his wrists were bandaged.

Pappoús! Alex called out. From now on he would always call Andreas *Pappoús*, whether his mother was there or not. What was important was that Andreas got better. What mattered was that Andreas knew he was a grandfather and that someone loved him.

Shhh, Lena tried to quiet him. He's sleeping.

Andreas opened his eyes. I'm not sleeping, he said.

Alex threw down the pillows and ran up to Andreas and hugged him. *Pappoús!* he said again.

Lena smiled uncertainly, reached out and touched the blankets around his feet. *Yeía sou,* she said. How are you?

Edáksi, edáksi. OK. He gave a small smile.

Are you in pain?

No. No. Not too much.

Marsoula went up to him and patted his hand. Brother, she said. She kissed the top of his head. She started weeping, quietly. Standing there, patting his hand over and over. Lena took in the blood-seeped cloth at his wrists. Marsoula looked beautiful and tragic standing there with her brother and Lena found it hard to watch. They looked alike and the resemblance moved her. For all their differences, for all their difficulties, they were family. Brother and sister.

Look what we have! Marsoula moved away from the bed

towards the basket of food. Blinking rapidly, hiding her tears from Andreas. Keftedes, *spanakórizo, eliés, tyrí* . . .

Andreas nodded and closed his eyes again.

Lena went out to try and find a doctor. She closed the curtain, took a deep breath and swallowed hard. A young woman in a white coat was walking towards her. She swept past Lena and into the cubicle.

Are you the doctor? asked Marsoula.

The woman in the white coat didn't answer. She consulted a chart. He's had a blood transfusion. He's weak, but he'll live. He must rest. The day after tomorrow he can go home.

That's all? asked Lena.

That's all.

You must change the sheets, the woman said. Feed him something.

Marsoula handed the doctor a small brown envelope. The doctor nodded and took the envelope and pushed back through the curtain without a word. As Lena shook out the pillows she could hear the doctor's heels echo hard, all the way down the corridor.

*

The next afternoon, rain kept them inside. They played Scrabble in Greek and in English. Marsoula taught Alex how to play draughts and backgammon.

Can't we get a TV? Occasionally when the weather was bad, the same question.

No.

221

We have one at home.

Here, we don't need a TV.

Alex grumbled and moaned and she could see he was not convinced.

When is *Pappoús* coming back?

Soon.

But why is he sick?

This was a difficult question. Lena didn't know how to answer in a way that would make sense to a child. She was still trying to make sense of it herself.

He just is, she said.

Alex seemed about to speak. Instead, he shifted pieces around on the Scrabble board, making nonsense words, ending the game. He stood up and kicked at the board with his foot. Letters scattered across the floor.

Alex!

Andreas is sad, he said. I know. He stood there with his hands on his hips, defiant, his eyes full, wanting them to tell him something different.

*

The next evening, Kiria Maria and her granddaughter Kiki came to visit. They sat and had coffee on the top balcony. Marsoula was at church down in the *Hóra*, lighting candles for Andreas.

You are melancholic? Kiria Maria suddenly asked. *Móni sou?* Alone?

No. No. I'm OK, Lena smiled. She didn't know whether the

neighbour meant her lack of a husband or the fact that her father was in hospital.

And your father?

He'll be home soon.

Kalá.

You are a dancer? Kiki the granddaughter asked.

She hesitated. I teach dance now.

Oh, Kiki said. Your father told us you were the dancer.

Kiria Maria looked at Lena. You could stay. You could teach here.

Teach? She paused. On the island?

Your father thinks this is the good idea.

He said that?

Nai.

Lena couldn't quite believe it.

We have no dance teacher, Kiria Maria said. There is no school. But you could teach at the gymnasium.

You've given this some thought, Lena smiled.

It is the idea of Andreas.

I guess he has lots of ideas, Lena said, astonished. *He just doesn't share them with me.* She took a sip of coffee. It's an idea, she conceded. It's a possibility.

You should think on it.

I will, she said.

Thinking about dance, thinking about what Andreas had said, she inadvertently started to move. She stretched out her feet and pointed her toes several times.

Óla edáksi? asked Kiria Maria.

223

Too much coffee, smiled Lena. But it wasn't that.

Andreas had told them she was a dancer. That she could teach dance here.

She felt as if she were a small child performing for the first time and she could hear his distant applause, reverberating down the years, something she'd never expected or thought possible; something she could hold on to.

There was a photograph of Lena's first performance. She was in a tutu, smiling brightly. In her mind, Lena held the photo up close and examined it. She could see immediately what her teachers had seen. The child Lena had perfect alignment; she stood with her feet turned out and her back straight, her tailbone slightly turned under. Her collarbones stood out. She seemed to radiate energy. Lena thought: yes, the girl had something.

There was the temptation to turn away from this child-self, so full of the future.

Instead, Lena thought: When I get back, I must find a place for that photo.

Andreas discussing her life with his neighbours. Andreas wanting her to stay.

She smiled to herself as she lifted the coffee cup, something she'd done a million times, and looked at the angle of her fingers, the bend of her elbow. The beginnings of something took shape. This was her way of being in the world, she realized. Whatever form the dance took. Teaching. Choreography. It didn't matter. As a child she hadn't joined a ballet class for the usual pink and prettiness. She'd joined because she had to. Because it was in her to move. She felt reassured. She felt a strange surge of confidence.

Change the head roll. Return to the beginning of the movement, drop the head down.

She could see it, this dance unfolding in her mind. She could see herself surrounded by kids; demonstrating the steps, counting out the beats. She could see the children's faces, glowing, eager, brave. And for the first time ever, the image didn't pull a sense of failure in its wake, but a sense of accomplishment. A sense of direction.

Imagine yourself as bamboo, she'd tell the kids. There'd been a pot of bamboo out on the back veranda when she was small. She'd shared her mother's fascination with it. On days when it was very windy, on days when Catherine felt well enough to get out of bed, she would stand at the window and call her over: Look at the bamboo, Lena. How it bends in the wind. How it bends and doesn't break.

The mature fruit ripens close to the tree. She'd been told that too, by her mother, wanting to keep her close. But what if the fruit rots on the vine? Falls too close to the tree? She'd feared that. Puzzled over it. What if the fruit is flung far and wide by winds and storms? Can a person ever find their way back? It seemed to her, for the first time, that maybe it was possible.

Because in that moment, with Andreas in hospital and everything uncertain, she realized that she *had* actually built a life. Something solid, something she was good at and that she could go back to. It came to her, the selfish, unbidden thought: *I have a life in Australia.*

10

Alex wanted his grandfather back. He wanted to be with him again. Since Johnny's death and since his mother's operation he'd wanted a more settled life. He wanted his mother to be well and happy and not sad all the time. He'd been determined to enjoy himself here on this island with this new grandfather. For a time, this had worked. And now they were not happy. He didn't know how to make things better. At night he asked for the desk lamp to be left on in the study, something he hadn't needed since they'd come to the village. One night he wet the bed.

He had his own private grief and sadness which Lena glimpsed occasionally when he woke from nightmares, or asked her about dying, or said that he didn't want her to be away from him for too long. Apart from these times he protected her from what he was really feeling, as she protected him. That was what parents and children did, it seemed to her. It was part of the dance of family.

She sensed that Andreas was protecting her from something.

Andreas stayed a few days longer in the clinic because his blood pressure was very low, the doctor said. He was too weak. They must wait for the transfusion to take effect.

It was the first of May and a public holiday when Andreas was finally allowed home.

It was the day when Greeks shed their dark winter clothes. The wheat was turning from green to gold, high in the fields. The sound of bouzoúki rose up from parties in the village. A boy rode past on a bicycle with a bunch of carnations. The older Greeks were up in the mountains collecting wildflowers to make wreaths. Marsoula had gone with Kiria Sofia and Alex early that morning, baskets in hand. *For Andreas*, she said. When they got back with their baskets full Marsoula showed them how to make the *stefáni*. Getting Alex to bend the twigs and twist the wire around. They put wreaths on all the doors and wound flowers around the posts of the lower balcony.

Pappoús! Today, he's coming home!

That's right, Lena said. He's coming home.

Lena marvelled at the way the child lived in the present. The island was home now. It all seemed so simple.

Meanwhile, Lena had been up scouring the house. She'd cleaned all the windows and floors. She rubbed at the taps until they shone. She made sure that everything was in order, wanting it to be pristine. *I'm turning into my mother,* she thought. She washed the marble floors and reorganized the cupboard. All this activity, she thought it would take her mind off things, but she still felt off balance. She'd snapped at Alex over breakfast. She'd dropped a plate while she was washing up and cracked a glass on the tap.

She hung out the washing and across the street saw old

Giorgos digging an irrigation trench for the vines, running a hose down to the fields from his house.

Cars went past with garlands attached to windscreens and roof racks. Horns sounding. It was the first of May and it would soon be summer. Andreas was coming home but she didn't feel like celebrating.

Alex wanted to go to the clinic with Marsoula but Lena decided they should stay. We'll get everything nice, she said. We'll be the welcome party. But in her mind already she was walking down a long corridor far away from here. When Andreas returned, they would leave soon after. She'd rung work in Australia to ask for a few more weeks. Her birth father, she said. He's very ill.

The thought of leaving. She didn't know how she would raise this with Andreas. She felt that she was deserting him when he needed her and the thought flashed through that perhaps she was doing it on purpose. This brought her up sharp. She was always confounding herself.

Alex kept running up and down the steps. Full of nervous energy.

She stood out on the top balcony waiting for the taxi. She stood there watching as Marsoula opened the side door and helped Andreas out. He looked smaller and thinner as if he'd shrunk into himself.

Alex didn't hesitate. Lena watched him run downstairs, so excited to see his grandfather. A puppy let off its leash. He ran to Andreas and did not hold back. He'd found the *kombolói* beads –

the gift from the old man in Piraeus – and he thought that Andreas might like them. *Pappoús*, he said, holding up the beads. Look! he said. Andreas took the beads and leant forward to kiss him.

Andreas walked slowly up the steps. He stood there with Marsoula on one arm and Alex on the other. He looked at everything as if it were new. As if he'd been away a long time.

He stopped to look at the small square of garden. Lena held herself taut, arms crossed. She'd swept the rubber leaves into tight bundles, trimmed the bougainvillea, cut back the hibiscus.

It's good, he said. Looking up at the balcony he saw her and he called out. *The garden*. He smiled. *Is very good*. He stopped to admire the jasmine trailing the lower balcony. The wreath over the door. He stood looking at a small olive tree in a terracotta pot.

It's a present for you, she called out. He stood still, admiring the tiny olive tree.

They walked up the remaining stairs and Lena stepped forward as if onto a stage and gave him a hug. He hugged her back. Then they stood apart almost shyly. Up until now, they'd expressed affection through Alex. They'd expressed everything through the child. But something was different with her father returning to his house. As if the tectonic plates of their relationship had shifted. With a shock she realized that the change was in her: she was different.

Welcome home, she said.

He nodded and kept his eyes down.

Sharing the house with his daughter and his grandson. How quickly he'd become accustomed. How quickly the human being adapts. They had staved off the thunder of night-voices and the harsh terrain of the kitchen. They'd kept him away from himself. He had responsibilities to this daughter and grandson. It came to him with force now: *They kept him alive.*

Was this true? he asked himself. *Could this really be true?*

Lena thought that he was about to cry. She brushed away her own tears and reached out for his other arm and together with Marsoula and Alex they walked into the house.

*

There was a moment in Andreas' story when words failed him. He could not yet bring himself to tell of names given and withheld; of consequences. But he could start with this.

He pushed back from the table and stood up.

Here. He raised first one foot and then another. And here.

He stood like a man crucified. His hands outstretched. They made me stand this way and that.

Here. He pointed to the scar at the base of his spine, and here – he pointed to the back of his neck.

Finally he rolled up his shirtsleeves to show the burn marks. Here.

Lena pointed to the cuts on his inner wrist.

No, he said. He wasn't ready to speak about that.

Watching him make an inventory of his body, Lena felt a jolt of recognition: words were not enough. She'd sat quietly smoking during his story. She thought about the times as a young dancer she'd complained after a long day of rehearsal, *This is murder. This is torture.* She would never use such words again.

It's so recent, she said, carving into the silence. The Junta. Forty years is not so long ago.

Forty years is nothing, he said. In human history, it is the blink of an eye.

Andreas smoked another cigarette. You are upset?

I'm upset that you went through it.

He shrugged. Some scars fade. Some scars stay. A cigarette burn, for example – it stays. He lifted his shirtsleeves again. Circular scars rose in an uneven line along the forearm. He sighed. He did not mention how the house changed aspect in the dark. He did not mention the night terrors. Of the names told and not told. He did not say how the house became its opposite, no longer a safe place. He did not tell of the everyday weapons concealed in the cutlery drawer. He offered no explanations.

For her part, she wondered how he'd been able to survive all these years. She knew what the body was capable of. She knew, as a dancer, the great swathes of endurance beyond fatigue. How to keep going. When to press hard and when to ease off: the point at which you could experiment with the body. To torture someone you had to know these things and ignore them. You had to push a person beyond words.

It came to her: the torturer and the artist shared similar under-standings.

He gestured around the kitchen. He pointed towards the cupboard. You have cleaned everything?

All organized. She smiled at him.

Good, he said. Very good.

*

It was a clear, blue-wash morning. She stretched out. She'd got up late, opened the shutters and watched Kirios Giorgos ploughing the fields with his donkey. Yesterday, walking up in the mountains behind the village, she'd seen two men doing the same thing. A hand plough, attached to the donkey, the man walking behind. It reminded her of the first time she'd seen Andreas. Just over three months ago.

Everything was on a loop now. Everything reminding her of that first day in the village. How she'd stood at the edge of the field, waiting.

They would be going soon and she was determined to imprint everything. Memorize it as she'd once been able to memorize whole dances.

Alex had been up for a while. The floor was strewn with toy cars. His Nintendo stuck between cushions. He'd opened the door and was down on the front steps, hitting at the step with a bamboo stick. She called to him, and he came running and gave her a hug.

How long have you been up?

A long time, he said.

Why didn't you wake me? You always wake me.

You were tired, he said. With a knowledge beyond his years, he added, You needed to sleep.

She was moved by this. *Who was the adult and who was the child?*

Have you eaten anything? she asked.

No.

Let's eat, she said and took him by the hand and they climbed the steps with the sun on their backs, Alex hitting each step with his stick.

Andreas was up and at the stove with the *bríki*. Making coffee. Marsoula was off in the *Hóra* getting fresh bread. They were into a different rhythm now. Lena swept the house after her morning coffee, after the fruit and yoghurt and honey. She helped Marsoula with the cooking. Andreas did not go down to the fields.

My work can wait, he said.

She worried that he had so little energy. She worried that they would be going soon.

Mid-week they were invited to lunch at Kiria Maria's. Andreas decided not to come. He was too tired, he said.

When they arrived, Kirios Giannis was sitting on his front steps carving the seeds from a pumpkin, laying them on a tray, ready to be dried and salted. Kiria Maria was inside at the stove, frying the pumpkin into keftedes – *kolokithokeftédes* – for lunch. Here on the island, Lena saw that the older Greeks never wasted a thing. Andreas was no exception. He salvaged all their scraps for the animals or for compost. Everything could be used. Despite their cars and mobile phones, the older people still lived a life very close to the land. A few of the men still went into the *Hóra* on donkeys. They were largely self-sufficient. She could understand why Andreas admired them. Had learnt from them.

But where is your father? Kiria Maria had a concerned look on her face.

He's resting. Lena paused. He's still very tired.

We are worried for him.

Lena nodded. When they were all sitting down, Kiria Maria feeding them, Lena asked, What was it like here, in the old days?

Without cars, Kirios Giannis said, no electricity, only donkeys. Ten years ago, in the *Hóra*, we had donkeys still, to help with the rubbish. Then we sent all our donkeys to Santorini, he laughed. For the Americans.

Lena thought of the cruise ships decanting tourists at Santorini. The photos she'd seen of people loaded onto donkeys struggling up the steps from the harbour to the town. People who should really have taken the funicular. Huge people on small animals.

And before that?

The Occupation? During the Second World War they came to the island . . .

Kiria Maria put the bread on the table. We still know Italian words, she said. We are children when they come. I was small. We were hungry all the time. She wrinkled her nose. They stole our hens. They stole our vegetables. The Italians – no better than the Germans. But sometimes, she paused, as if to reconsider, the Italians – they gave sweets to the children.

They took all we had from the farms, Giannis said. We had nothing to eat. We all knew to collect greens, to get the rabbits. Everyone: women and children up in the mountains. We ate what we could find.

And the years after that? Lena ventured carefully. The 1960s and 1970s? Life under the Junta?

The Junta? Kiria Maria looked over at her husband.

Kirios Giannis put down his soup spoon and held up his fist. Strong, he said. Was good!

Really? Lena tried to hide her surprise. *Yiatí?* Why?

Then old Kirios Giannis bent back to his soup: silent, uncomfortable, sad, as if he'd been caught out in some way, and Kiria Maria emerged from the galley kitchen again with a steaming plate of *spanakórizo* and changed the subject.

The jail! she exclaimed, a quick glance at her husband. She sensed his upset. Two men escaped!

On Naxos? Lena was confused. During the Junta?

Óxi, óxi, Maria said. *Tóra*. Now!

Giannis looked up. He'd recovered himself. Last night – on the news. They knew that Andreas didn't have a television.

Kiria Maria moved attention away from her husband and his views on the Junta and instead they discussed the prison escape by two armed men. They are dangerous! This was their second escape from the same prison in Thessaloniki. She shook her head. Both times by helicopter!

One a Greek, the other Albanian, Kiria Maria said. *Alvanós*, she muttered again.

Lena knew that Albanians were blamed for all the problems in Greece and couldn't resist. But the main man is Greek? she said. And the people helping him, she paused, are Greek?

Nai, Kiria Sofia conceded. But with an *Alvanós*! She emphasized the word for Lena's benefit.

The *Alvanós* or the gypsy, said Kirios Giannis, reaching for the bread. Always the same problem.

*

When they got back from the meal, Andreas was out on the balcony with a blanket around his feet, looking out to sea. A book of poems by Cavafy face down on the table. Next to this, a small screwdriver and Alex's toy truck, now restored.

Would you like coffee? she asked. Anything?

No, no, he said. Your meal was good?

Very good, she said.

They have the big heart, said Andreas. Maria and Giannis.

Yes, she said.

They sat a while in silence. Lena went to get them both a glass of water and when she came back she said: Kirios Giannis says life was good under the Junta . . .

Ax! Andreas adjusted the blanket at his feet. Some people say this. The strong leader. He tried to laugh but coughed instead. The big myth. People long for it. And I can understand . . .

You can?

Vévea. Of course. The father. The mother. The Church. We

want to be told how to live. We want order. We fear chaos. We fear our own freedom.

But life is chaos . . .

Akrivós. Exactly.

They sat in silence and then she said: You know we have to leave.

I know. He lifted a hand from the blanket and gestured out across the fields. How will you live without the donkey, the cockerel?

You're making fun of me.

No, he smiled. Never.

He sat up a little straighter in the chair, turned to her. Tell me – did you find a key? In the cupboard?

I found a key in the drawer.

Oh, he said. So that's what happened.

You don't remember?

Not exactly.

Everything was a mess in the cupboard.

And the key in the drawer?

Yes, she said.

Where is the key now?

On a shelf. She hesitated. Do you need it?

No. I don't need it any more. I don't need it, he repeated. He lay back against the chair and closed his eyes. You came here to be disappointed.

I'm not disappointed. I'm upset, she said, biting her lip.

Why?

We have to leave.

You were always going to leave, he said. Always.

She waited for him to say more, but they sat in silence as the sun went down over Paros, listening to the children's voices and the cicadas starting up, conscious of the things unsaid between them.

In the last weeks, they spent a lot of time on the balcony. They were sheltered by the mountain and had their own microclimate. High up here in her father's house with the rubber tree shading the terrace, she felt as if she were in a rainforest in North Queensland. Through a gap in the trees she could see a line of eucalypts beyond the village. A reminder of Australia. In the mornings, Andreas liked to sit on the lower balcony where it was cooler. Lena often joined him. They would sit and watch the first haze of bumblebees in the heat. Summer was pushing through now. Orange butterflies soared past and she could hear a melodic whistle like a bell bird and a rustle in the trees.

One morning Lena saw Kiria Sofia bent double walking down one of the paths, stooping to cut greens.

What's she doing? she asked Andreas.

Collecting *hórta*. Andreas turned to Lena. Now is the best time. He stood up slowly, putting the blanket aside. Since his return from hospital he always felt cold. Come, he said. I will show you. He went upstairs and Lena followed him. He went straight to the unlocked drawer and took out a knife. He held the knife in his palm and tested its weight. Lena watched him, anxious. She stood biting her lip. She almost put out a hand to stop him, to get him to put the knife back. He turned and caught the expression on her face.

Min anisihís! he said. Don't worry! Let's go.

As they walked up the path behind the house, Andreas stopped for a rest every so often. Lena picked leaves from the edge of the path.

Is this *hórta*?

No. No. Andreas laughed. This is poison! He threw Lena's handful into the road. Let me show you. Come! And with his knife he foraged in a neighbour's field and cut what looked like dandelion weeds. He cut three different kinds of leaves from three separate plants and explained the difference.

This – he pointed to the slightly furry leaves – is *pikrós*, bitter. This – he showed slightly smaller, pointed leaves, a different shade of green – is *gliká*, sweet. *Óla mazí*, he said. *Nóstimo!*

You cook them all together?

Nai. Óla mazí, he repeated. Lena then went with him around the village, trying to identify leaves from small patches of land, watching Andreas' face for the click of the tongue and the raised chin, which meant no, or the Bravo! when she got it right.

Lena thought that she would only ever be able to identify one kind of leaf – the kind that looked liked dandelion. Her eye wasn't practised enough. It would take years, she thought, to become so accomplished.

The *hórta* is only until May, cautioned Andreas. After, is too *pikrós*. It is the young leaves which are best. It was the first time she'd seen him so energized since his return. It was the opportunity to teach her something, she realized, to share knowledge with her.

The next day Lena decided to collect *hórta* by herself. To show what she'd learnt. She left Alex with Andreas and went out into the mountains with her knife and she stayed out in the last of the sun. At first she wasn't sure, between the riot of clover and daisies and wild dill frothing the side of the path. She cut slowly, a leaf here and there, trying to remember what Andreas had said.

After two hours she had a large bag of leaves which she knew would boil down to a plateful and she felt as light and empty as if she'd been dancing all day; she'd been so involved in the work. Then the ritual of cleaning and cutting. So much work for so little food. She thought of all the older people in the village during the war; people all over Greece – taking to the hills, literally, digging for greens, shooting rabbits, trying to stay alive.

Andreas, trying to stay alive.

She stood looking around the fields blurred with wildflowers. Her nails full of dirt and a bag of greens at her feet. The things she'd known in life up until now had been very different.

She'd understood the relation of shoulder to hip. She'd understood joints and tendons. She knew how the leg lengthened and where it started from. She could tell you how to stretch and hold and release a muscle. She could teach how to lower the ribs and pull up the pelvis. But she knew little about the world outside the body. The world of other growing things. Being here on the island had thrown her open to this other world. Andreas had thrown her open to this other world. Only now did she realize how much she would miss it.

*

It was almost June. Tomorrow an Albanian would come, said Andreas. He would come with the tractor to help plough the fields. Andreas showed Lena how to pick the best chamomile and dry it on the baking tray. She sifted it by hand every day for a week. She went with Andreas into the fields to watch him gather herbs. Andreas on his knees down in a patch of strawberries. His wrists were no longer bandaged. He was confident when he reached out into the earth. With a twist he yielded spring onions and lettuce. He held out a stick and told the hissing geese to go, get lost, *fíge*!

After the fields had been dug he returned to inspect the work. Lena went with him. She was pleased to see that each day he was doing more.

Andreas lifted his stick, warning off the geese, and without looking at her he said: You have rung your mother?

For a moment, she didn't answer. She'd only rung Australia twice since coming here.

You should ring your mother.

And say what?

That soon you will be home.

She still hadn't booked tickets. And ringing her mother was

the last thing Lena wanted to do. She couldn't bear to explain everything when she was still trying to absorb it herself.

She'll know soon enough.

She is your family, he said.

And you're not?

At this, he turned away. He threw the stick aside and started walking up towards the house. She followed him.

She told you only that I disappeared? he called this over his shoulder. She thought I was with the other woman?

That's right.

Nothing about prison?

No.

Lena didn't know why he was raking through it again.

There was a strained pause and then he said, Let me tell you something. The Greek woman, she never came back. He stopped for breath and sat on a low stone wall.

I don't get it.

She, too, was disappeared. She'd been training to be a lawyer, helping Mandilaras – the lawyer of Papandreou. In opposition to the Junta. But Mandilaras never came back. They found his body on Rhodos. He was the lawyer for human rights, born here, on this island. There's a statue to him in his village of Koronos. One day, I could show you. He paused and wiped his hand across his eyes. She was disappeared.

But . . . Lena was confused. What happened to her?

She became extreme. Involved in all sorts of groups. He does not say that he feels responsible for her disappearance; for telling her name. He is not yet ready to say that. He says nothing of the man Vasilis who'd hunted her down. He says nothing of dreams or hopes or nightmares in which Irini appears and disappears or arrives unannounced in front of him, a dead woman, unable to forgive. He takes a deep breath.

She went to prison. She was tortured. His voice cracked. When she came out, she was changed. She was even more Left. Eventually, she was killed.

In prison?

No. He closes his eyes. Then, for the first time, he says it out loud. In Athens. In the street.

My God.

She was putting a bomb . . .

Andreas went silent.

You loved her? She felt a pang of something on her mother's behalf.

Yes, he said.

This is difficult.

Yes.

She felt inadequate to comfort him. She wanted to put out a hand. To soothe and steady. Instead, she drew back, unsettled. The way a story turns, a life turns. She desperately wanted a cigarette.

Lipáme, I'm sorry, she said. I truly am.

When such things happen, the whole of life is suddenly different, he said. All changed. My view of politics. Of people. Of myself. The *kamáki* – even he changes. Andreas wanted to leave the subject of Irini. Your mother wrote to Marsoula. When I came back from Makrónisos, my sister showed me this letter, asked if it was true. I was with many *xéni*, I told her. But I wrote to your mother. I wrote that I did not want to be a father to this child. I could not come to Australia. I never heard nothing after that.

Until now.

Yes, he said. Until now.

But you knew about me, she said. It came out as a statement, an accusation.

Yes. *Vévea*. Of course. After you are born, I knew. But I didn't love her . . .

For God's sake, Andreas! You didn't have to love her. Lena wanted to say, *You only had to love me*. She felt needy and ashamed. She said: Many fathers still contribute . . .

And many do not. He stood up again. I did not.

He never flinched from saying the difficult thing. She could almost admire him for it.

He could see her face set against him. He threw up his hands, exasperated. You had the good life, he said. The stepfather loved you. Your mother loved you. It is time now . . . he stopped himself, wondering whether he should go on.

Time for what?

To grow up, he said sharply.

Jesus! she said.

He would not stop there. You share the defect with your mother . . .

Oh, she said, her voice hard. What would that be?

You do not see the good for what it is. And when change comes – as it must – you cannot let go.

She flushed at the truth of it.

I zoí íne roí, he said simply.

Life is flow?

Yes, he said.

And yet you can't say, *my daughter* in public?

He stared at her, shocked, and then laughed. Bravo, you have me!

It's not difficult.

The words are not important, he said.

She put her hands on her hips. You're a contradictory bastard, you know that?

A smile crossed his face.

I'll see you later, she said, and moved quickly up the path, away from him.

Kaliníhta, he called after her. They were both near to the house now and he frowned as he heard the backs of her sandals hitting the steps, years of rebuke or so it seemed to him, hitting hard against the marble stairs.

*

Alex was playing outside the house with a group of children. She called to him and when he refused to come in she raised her voice. Now, kiddo. Bedtime.

But . . . He looked forlornly at the other children who would be allowed to stay up much later.

No buts. Now. She took him by the hand and dragged him upstairs. He could see that she was upset and that it was nothing to do with him.

Were you fighting with *Pappoús*?

No, she said.

I heard voices.

Shhh, kiddo. Quiet now. It was nothing. She made him brush his teeth and led him to his bed in the study. She kissed the top of his head and drew back the curtain. Sleep well, she said.

She paced around the kitchen, filled the *bríki* and boiled water for chamomile tea, feeling furious. When she got down to her room she sat on the bed taking small sips, trying to calm herself. His words could sting, no two ways about it. Her way of looking at the world – she was her mother's daughter – how could she change? Accept that she'd had a good innings as a dancer. Accept that she'd never have another child and that one day this longing would stop? She went to stand against the rail in the bathroom. Some stretches would help. She raised her leg high. She did the other side. She concentrated on her breathing. She stretched up as high as she could on her toes, extending her arms overhead. She felt a pull on her left side, around the scar. It hurt much less than before. She put a towel down on the marble floor and did some forward bends until she felt calmer, then she washed her face and brushed her teeth and climbed into bed and wept long and hard into her pillow.

*

When she woke the next morning, her eyes were swollen. She pressed a cold flannel against her eyelids. She splashed cold water on her face, put on her sunglasses and sunscreen and went down to the phone box to ring Catherine. The dog was gone; Andreas had got up early for the first time since his return. *They must be in the fields,* she thought.

She took out the phone card and held the receiver under her chin as she dialled the number.

Hello? The line crackled and her mother sounded a long way off. Lena braced herself.

It's me, Lena.

How are you? Her mother sounded genuinely pleased to hear her voice.

We're fine. Lena paused. Well, not everyone. Not exactly. Andreas ...

Her mother cut in: What's wrong with him?

He's been ill. Lena decided not to tell the whole story.

He's getting on, said Catherine. He's no spring chicken.

No, he isn't.

That's why we'll be back a little later. That's why I haven't rung ...

More time off work?

It's not a problem.

Leave without pay? Lena knew that her mother fretted about her finances.

It's fine. The school were good. When have I ever had time off?

That's true, her mother said. Only now. They can't hold it against you. And Alex?

He's great. He loves it here. He doesn't want to leave. Lena took a deep breath. There's something I need to ask.

OK. Lena could hear the unease in her mother's voice.

It's about Andreas.

Uh-huh.

Why didn't you tell me he'd been in prison?

Would it have made a difference?

I think so, yes.

How?

Just. A bigger picture.

It wouldn't have changed anything.

That's exactly what he said.

Well, then.

Not that it was an excuse. Lena tried to soften, for her mother's sake.

No.

But, she pushed, why didn't you tell me?

Catherine went silent and then cleared her throat. Andreas broke my heart.

But Johnny! Lena protested. He loved you to bits.

I know that, said Catherine.

What, then? Lena held her breath, fearful of the answer.

It wasn't enough.

There, her mother had said it. The force of it like a blow.

I had big ideas when I was young, Catherine said. Travelling the world, fresh out of college. Then I got to Greece. Fell in love with Andreas, thought I'd stay. She gave a dry laugh. Marry him, have kids: the whole kit-and-caboodle.

Live in Greece? Lena was astonished. I've never heard you say that before.

Catherine sighed. Instead, I came back here. Unmarried, pregnant. Catholic. Imagine! Without Johnny, it would've been so much worse.

You kept it all to yourself. You took to your bed.

I still take to my bed. Her mother's voice was strained. When are you coming back?

Soon, Lena said.

Good.

But, for the record – he's not a complete bastard.

You can be the judge of that.

But I grew up thinking that he was. As if this was all there was to him.

You want me to apologize? Her mother's voice hardened. Look, Lena, I did the best I could.

I don't want you to apologize, Lena said. She stood helplessly, not knowing what she wanted.

Look, she said to her mother, the line's bad, I'll ring you again soon. A cement truck roared past and Lena really couldn't hear a thing. Goodbye, she said, and without waiting for an answer, put the phone down.

She leant back against the phone box, exhausted. That wasn't so bad, she said to herself. They'd covered more ground in that

one phone call than they had in a lifetime. *A grown-up thing to do.*
She trudged back up the path to Andreas' house, trying to make
sense of family, its slippery contours and combinations, what she
expected from it: what it would never deliver.

*

The bougainvillea was out. The poppies along the road were
wilting. A wave of rock irises and rock roses emerged to take their
place.

Figs covered the ground. They baked small and terracotta-hard
in the sun. No matter how many she tried to collect, her bicycle left a trail of green and yellow along the path. There were fine
wisps of blossom on the olive trees and Andreas bought four basil
pots to ward off insects.

The days were violently blue and sunny. They started going to
the beach at Agios Giorgos every afternoon. She was conscious
that these were the last days on the island. The beach was shallow and they had to walk out past the sandbar. When the wind
was up Alex loved to bodysurf. She would hold him up high in
the water and launch him off. He would hold his arms out in
front and put his head down, start paddling. Occasionally he got
dumped. In the waves she felt that he was all bones and thinness.
Her feet slid under the weight of the water and the shifting sand
and seaweed. She kept trying to keep him afloat. That was her
job, she knew. It would always be her job.

She sat on the beach watching the sunset. Alex next to her.
She took her son's small feet in her hands. His second toe was

longer than the first. He'd have all sorts of problems later on, she thought. Her own feet were quite different. Her first and second toes were the same length – she remembered her childhood classes in the town hall, how the teacher had remarked on her feet, on her arches, exclaimed over her wonderful toes – perfect for dancing *en pointe*. Well, her son wouldn't be a dancer, she thought. Although he loved to move and run and stretch. The realization came with a sense of relief. All the striving for perfection. He would be spared that.

Andreas came down to join them one evening at sunset. They watched a small girl playing with her father at the water's edge. The child was running into the waves and out again, collecting water in a bucket, tipping the water at her father's feet.

Lena realized that she was looking at the little girl with enjoyment; delighting in the child's laughter and play. Her complicated feelings had shifted a little.

Andreas watched her closely. You wanted another child? he asked as gently as he could.

Lena frowned. By the time I knew, it was too late.

I'm sorry for this.

Me too. She was trying to be philosophical and was just about succeeding.

You have Alex.

I got lucky, she said, smiling.

You *are* lucky, said Andreas.

Alex leapt up – Watch this, *Pappoús*! He ran into the water and as soon as it got deeper, he dived down and did a handstand. He stood up and waved. They waved back.

Bravo! called Andreas. Very good.

Alex dived down again and came up spluttering.

Andreas stood up, just as the bright sun dissolved red into the water. Let's go, he said. He called to Alex, who insisted that they both witness one more handstand. Lena wrapped him in a towel and changed his shorts then they walked back up through town and Andreas paused outside a kafé. *Mía stigmí*, he said. He'd caught sight of the large television screen. Lena and Alex followed him in. It was a news broadcast. He stood there watching a while, hoping for disruption to the ferry services. Hoping for a riot in Athens. Hoping somehow to delay the departure of the girl and the grandson. But the news was about bribery and the Vatopedi monastery and whether Nea Dimokratia would survive the upcoming election or whether George Papandreou – the grandson of the Papandreou of his youth – would get in.

It was a warm evening and Andreas was subdued as he drove them back to the village in the truck. Lena noticed that the fields were dry and shorn of wheat. Brown bales stood in the centre of brown fields. Potato crops formed pyramids, like stone cairns, waiting to be transported. It was the beginning of June. It was summer.

It was time to go.

She stood at the port, waiting. Alex kept scanning back through the people, through the cars and trucks, looking for his grandfather.

Where is he, Mama?

He may not come, said Lena. She felt wretched and her eyes were swollen. She'd cried herself to sleep.

But *why*?

It's just the way it is, kiddo.

They'd got up early and caught a taxi to the port. Before leaving, she'd called for Andreas, but the house had echoed back. His coffee cup was rinsed and dried, placed next to the sink. The ashtray had been emptied. The only signs that he had been up before them. Down at the harbour they sat near the Greek families, surrounded by hampers of cheese and ribboned boxes from the *zaharoplastío*. There were groups of tourists sitting on cases and rucksacks. Everyone sat in the shade of the concrete wall. The wind coming from the direction of the Portara and the sun gaining strength.

These past months, she thought. *What to make of them?* She wondered what she would remember of Andreas and of this visit: his abruptness, his twists and turns of mood. His inability to soften a blow. Then she recalled his tenderness with Alex. His attempts to care for her. The things he had been through.

She was relieved to see the ferry appear around the headland and busied herself with their tickets and bags.

The port police opened the gates and the old Greeks pushed their way through with their parcels. She adjusted her sunglasses to walk across the concourse. It was hot and in Melbourne now it would be winter. She struggled with her case and its recalcitrant wheels. She had a sudden ache for her stepfather. If only Johnny were still around, he would've fixed her suitcase. He would've said something to make it all better.

She walked slowly towards the ramp, then decided to turn again, to look at the island one last time, one last look at the Portara, and that was when she saw him hurrying towards the boat.

They'd argued the night before. Found fault with each other. She knew the pattern – had seen it with her mother many times. How it seemed easier to leave on bad terms, a justification for leaving, almost. Andreas had insisted on cooking although he didn't seem well. He had a bad cough and a slight fever. She'd been worried about him.

You should see a doctor, Andreas. She sounded too harsh. It came out all wrong.

He coughed again. No more doctors! I will never go to another doctor. He was adamant.

What if you are really sick?

I'm strong. I'm fit. He pounded his chest. He pointed to the cigarettes on the table. These are my only problem. He paused and smiled, then saw her serious face.

It's a big problem, she said. She thought of the cigarettes in her bag. When I get back to Australia, she promised herself, I'll give up for good.

It's my business, he said, annoyed. *Dinató potíri!* You should eat. You should not drink.

Not that again.

They both stared at each other. A mirror image of hands on hips. Something wounded in the eyes. Wondering how far to push, how to hold back, how to go forward.

Lena wondered if she would ever see him again. She bit her lip.

There was the urge to cry and she put down her wine glass. I must go and pack. She stood up suddenly, gathered her things and moved towards the door. Alex stood in his pyjamas watching them, holding the toy truck that Andreas had fixed. He could see what they were doing – hurting each other to make the pain go away. Adults had a big appetite for this. He walked towards Andreas and held up the truck. *Pappoús*, he said, trying to distract him. *Pappoús*, he tried again, but his grandfather didn't seem to notice.

Stay for coffee, Andreas appealed to Lena. He looked small and drawn standing under the fluorescent light in the kitchen. He hugged the child to him then moved towards the stove and picked up the *bríki*. One coffee! She noted the angry scars at his wrists. The old scars tracking up his arms.

She turned away from him. I haven't packed. Now she was the one unable to soften. She was the one withdrawing, like a small creature into its shell. We leave early, she said. Perhaps we should say goodbye now.

Andreas narrowed his eyes, unsure of what she meant. I know what time you leave, he said.

He was waiting for her to say something more. Some sign from her. He would take them to the port, he wanted to say. They could have coffee there. He would buy them breakfast. Beyond that, he couldn't bear to think. But there was something resolute about the daughter pushing him away and he stayed silent.

She put Alex to bed and then came back to say good night. They embraced stiffly at the front door and then he stood watching the shadow of his daughter lengthen down the steps. She did not turn back, even though he willed her to, and he did not call out, even though he wanted to, and he spent the night full of regret, wishing he could be different. Wishing he could find the right words.

*

The ferry horn sounded long and low and melancholy. Alex had also turned to look. He tugged at her sleeve. *Pappoús!*

Andreas was moving quickly towards them. He took his cap off and waved it high in the air. She paused as the ramp levered up and he got close enough that she could hear:

I kóri mou, he called out, first in Greek and then in English, My daughter.

And then more loudly so that everyone could hear, he called again as if nothing else mattered, waving until his hand hurt and the ferry disappeared and he could no longer see them, his voice ragged as the sea.

Author's Note

There are certain letters and sounds in the Greek alphabet which have no true equivalent in English. Greek is an inflected language and Greek masculine nouns ending in 'os', 'as', and 'is' lose the final 's' in the accusative case. However, to avoid confusion for English speakers, in this book Greek nouns retain the final 's' and Greek speech is rendered phonetically into English.

Acknowledgements

I would like to thank our friends in Greece as always for their hospitality and warmth.

In particular I want to thank the following people: Sofia, Giannis, Annoula and all the Skilaki family, Kaiti Pittara-Viska and Giannis Viska, Dr Margarita Lianou and family, Dr Ruth Macrides, Dr Tatiani Rapatzikou, Professor Ioannis Hassiotis, Katy Logotheti-Anderson and Kevin Anderson, Ourania Logotheti, Nikos and Astrid Mandilaras, Jackie and Themos Bogiatzoglou, Jennifer Custer and Vasilis Dimos, Jacqueline Morley and Natalie Garry.

Finally, thanks to my agent Bill Hamilton for his ongoing support and to my editor Bella Lacey and all at Granta for their encouragement, inspiration and hard work.